Greatest HITS of the 90s

55 Great Songs for EZ GUITAR

CW00337203

Project Manager: Aaron Stang
Music Editor: Colgan Bryan
Art Design: Carmen Fortunato

© 2000 WARNER BROS. PUBLICATIONS
All Rights Reserved

Any duplication, adaptation or arrangement of the compositions
contained in this collection requires the written consent of the Publisher.
No part of this book may be photocopied or reproduced in any way without permission.
Unauthorized uses are an infringement of the U.S. Copyright Act and are punishable by law.

14⁹⁹

CONTENTS

ARTIST INDEX

455 ROCKET

Words and Music by
GILLIAN WELCH and DAVE RAWLINGS

© 1994 IRVING MUSIC, INC. (BMI) and CRACKLIN' MUSIC (BMI)
All Rights Reserved

block a - live.   I could - n't hard - ly wait____   just to take

my turn.____   She was made   for____

____ the straight - a - ways,   she grew up hat - ing Chev - ro - lets.

1.

She's a rock - et,   she was made   to burn.____

2.

3.

____   Burn,____   Lord,____   she's a rock - et,

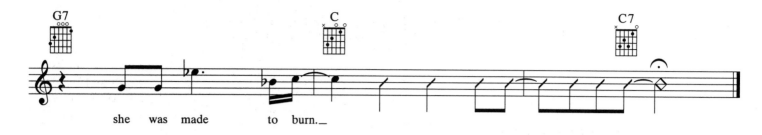

she was made to burn.___

Verse 2:
Whose juke pile piece of Chevelle is this?
You boys come here to race or just kiss?
Don't you want to know what I got underneath my hood?
I know she might sound like she's missing,
But, buddy, she could teach you a lesson.
In just a quarter mile, I'll smoke you good.

Chorus 2:
In my 455 rocket, the kind the police drive,
I couldn't hardly wait just to take my turn.
She was made for the straightaways,
She grew up hating Chevrolets.
She's a rocket, she was made to burn.

Verse 3:
I'm telling you and I ain't ashamed,
I cried when that wrecker came.
As we skid, I thought I heard the angels sing.
We hit the curve and began to sail,
Took out most of the safety rail.
Even the cop asked me,
"Man, what'd you have in that thing?"

Chorus 3:
I had a 455 rocket, the very kind you drive.
You ought to watch yourself when you take that turn.
'Cause she was made for the straightaways,
She grew up hating Chevrolets.
She's a rocket, she was made to burn.

6th AVENUE HEARTACHE

Words and Music by
JAKOB DYLAN

© 1996 WB MUSIC CORP. and BROTHER JUMBO MUSIC
All Rights Administered by WB MUSIC CORP.
All Rights Reserved

Verse 2:
Below me, there was a homeless man
Singing songs I knew complete.
On the steps alone, his guitar in hand.
His fifty years stood where he stands.
(To Chorus:)

Verse 3:
Walkin' home on those streets,
The river winds, they move my feet.
The subway steam, like silhouettes in dreams,
Stood by me, just like moonbeams.
(To Chorus:)

ALL I WANNA DO

Words and Music by
SHERYL CROW, WYN COOPER, KEVIN GILBERT,
BILL BOTTRELL and DAVID BAERWALD

© 1993, 1995 WARNER-TAMERLANE PUBLISHING CORP., OLD CROW MUSIC, WB MUSIC CORP.,
CANVAS MATTRESS MUSIC, IGNORANT MUSIC, ALMO MUSIC CORP. and ZEN OF INIQUITY
All Rights Reserved

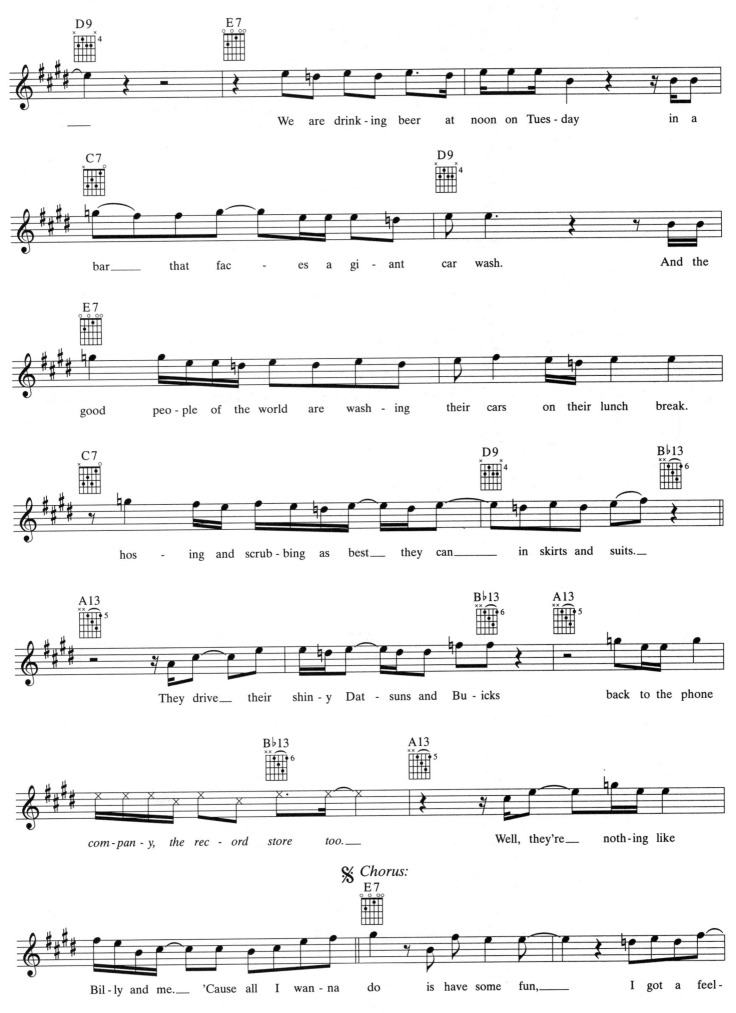

12

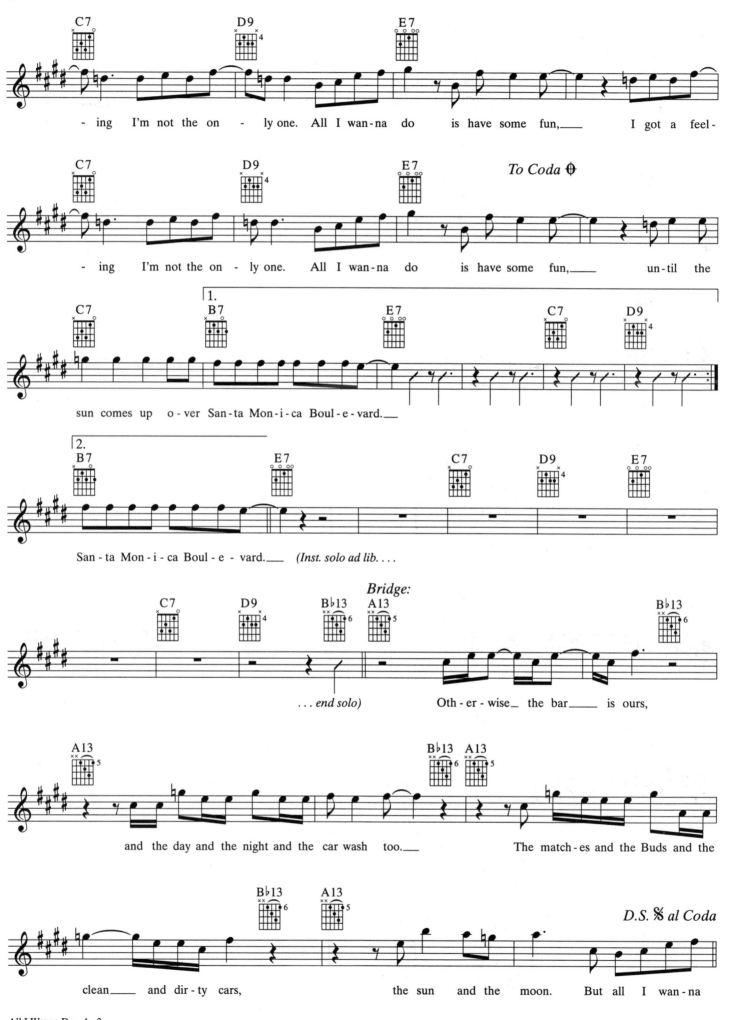

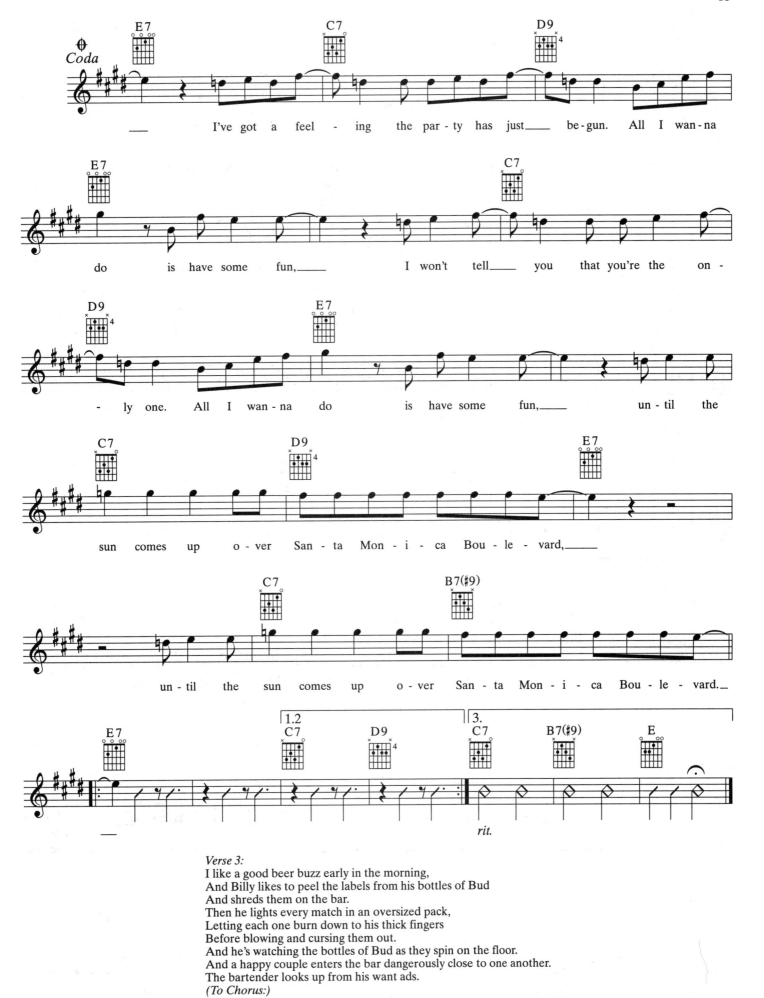

Verse 3:
I like a good beer buzz early in the morning,
And Billy likes to peel the labels from his bottles of Bud
And shreds them on the bar.
Then he lights every match in an oversized pack,
Letting each one burn down to his thick fingers
Before blowing and cursing them out.
And he's watching the bottles of Bud as they spin on the floor.
And a happy couple enters the bar dangerously close to one another.
The bartender looks up from his want ads.
(To Chorus:)

ALL STAR

Words and Music by
GREG CAMP

© 1999 WARNER-TAMERLANE PUBLISHING CORP. and SQUISH MOTH MUSIC
All Rights for SQUISH MOTH MUSIC Administered by WARNER-TAMERLANE PUBLISHING CORP.
All Rights Reserved

16

All Star - 4 - 3
GFM0001

Chorus:

Verse 3:
It's a cool place and they say it gets colder.
You're bundled up now, wait till you get older.
But the meteor men beg to differ,
Judging by the hole in the satellite picture.
The ice we skate is getting pretty thin.
The water's getting warm, so you might as well swim.
My world's on fire, how about yours?
That's the way I like it and I'll never get bored.
(To Chorus:)

Verse 4:
Somebody once asked, could I spare some change for gas.
I need to get myself away from this place.
I said, "Yep, what a concept;
I could use a little fuel myself
And we could all use a little change."
(To Verse 5:)

BREAKFAST AT TIFFANY'S

Words and Music by
TODD PIPES

© 1995, 1996 LORENE, LORENE MUSIC
All Rights Administered by WB MUSIC CORP.
All Rights Reserved

one thing we got._____   one thing we got._____

Ooh,_____   and   I_____

BRIAN WILSON

Words and Music by
STEVEN PAGE

© 1994 WB MUSIC CORP. and TREAT BAKER MUSIC
All Rights Administered by WB MUSIC CORP.
All Rights Reserved

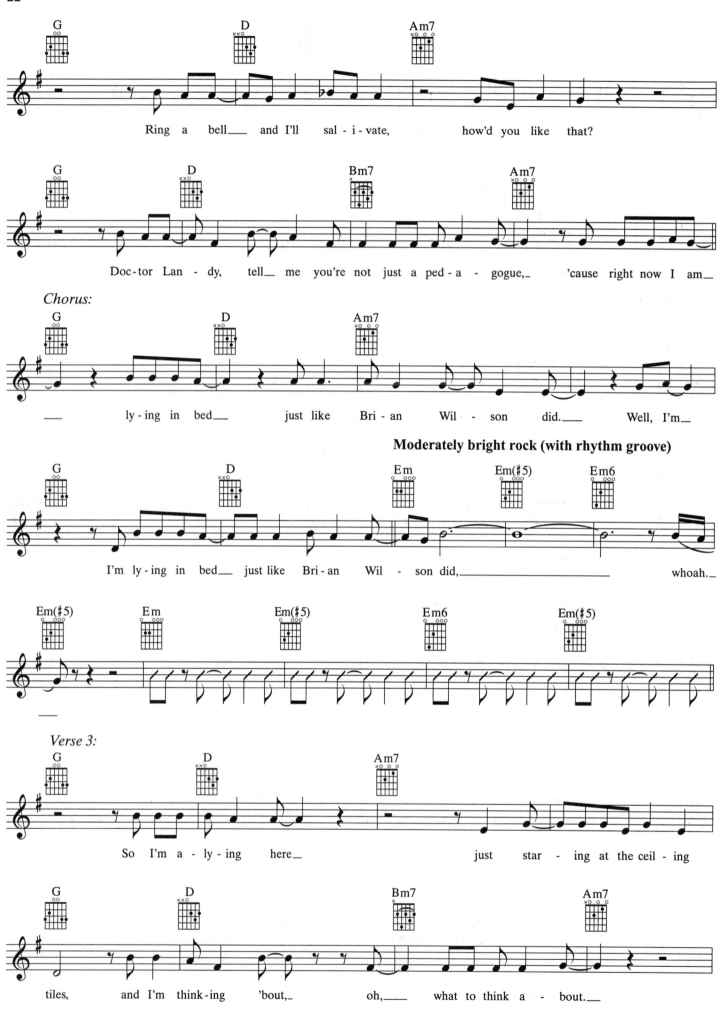

CHANGE THE WORLD

Words and Music by
TOMMY SIMS, GORDON KENNEDY
and WAYNE KIRKPATRICK

Moderately slow ♩ = 96

1. If I could reach the stars,⎯ I'd pull one down for you,⎯
2. If I could be a king,⎯ e - ven for a day,⎯

⎯ shine it on my heart⎯
⎯ I'd take you as my queen.⎯

so you could see the truth,⎯ that this love I have in - side⎯
I'd have it no oth - er way.⎯ And our love⎯ would rule⎯

© 1996 Universal - MCA Music Publishing, a Division of Universal Studios, Inc.,
Universal - PolyGram International Publishing, Inc., Sondance Kid Music,
BMG Songs, Inc and Careers - BMG Music Publishing, Inc.
All Rights for Sondance Kid Music Controlled and Administered by
Universal - PolyGram International Publishing, Inc.
All Rights Reserved

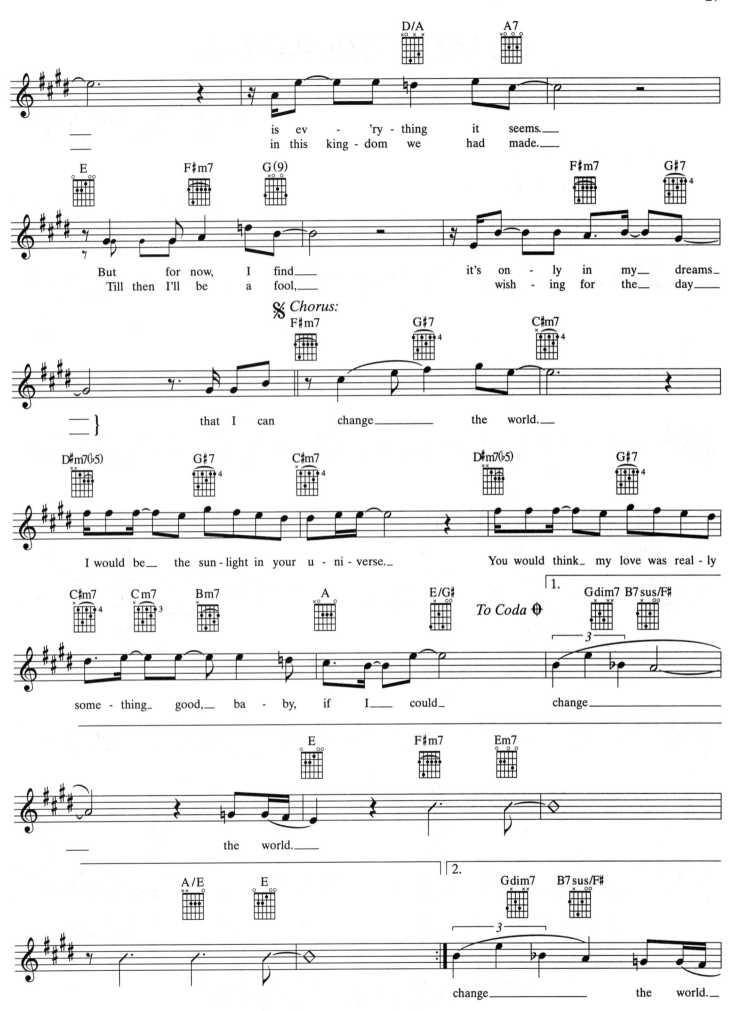

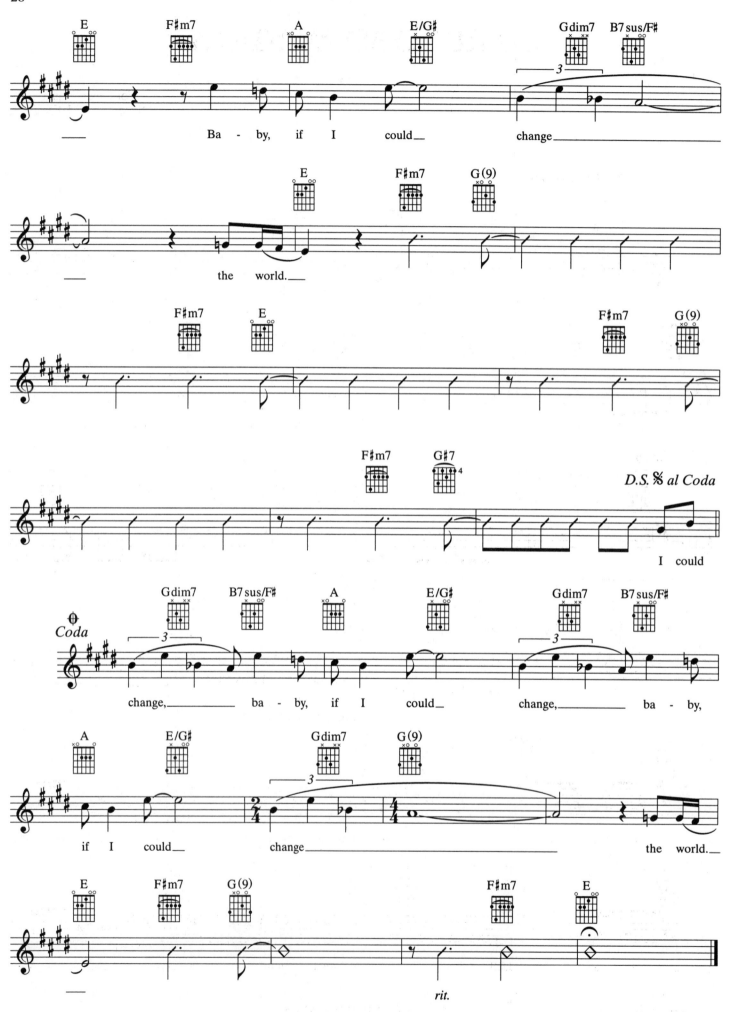

COME TO MY WINDOW

Words and Music by
MELISSA ETHERIDGE

© 1993 M.L.E. MUSIC, INC. (ASCAP)
All Rights Administered by ALMO MUSIC CORP. (ASCAP)
All Rights Reserved

Bridge:

I don't care_____ what_ they think._   I don't care_____ what_

_ they say._____   What do they know a-bout this_ love,_

an - y - way?_____

_____   Come,_

_____   come_ to my_ win-dow,   I'll_ be home,_   I'll_

D.S. 𝄋𝄋

_____ be home,_ I'll_ be home._   I'm com-ing home._____

Verse 2:
Keeping my eyes open, I cannot afford to sleep.
Giving away promises I know that I can't keep.
Nothing fills the blackness that has seeped into my chest.
I need you in my blood, I am forsaking all the rest.
Just to reach you,
Just to reach you.
Oh, to reach you.
(To Chorus:)

CONSTANT CRAVING

Words and Music by
k.d. lang and BEN MINK

© 1992 Zavion Music (Administered by Zomba Enterprises Inc.)
Universal - PolyGram International Publishing Inc. and Bumstead Productions U.S., Inc.
All Rights Reserved

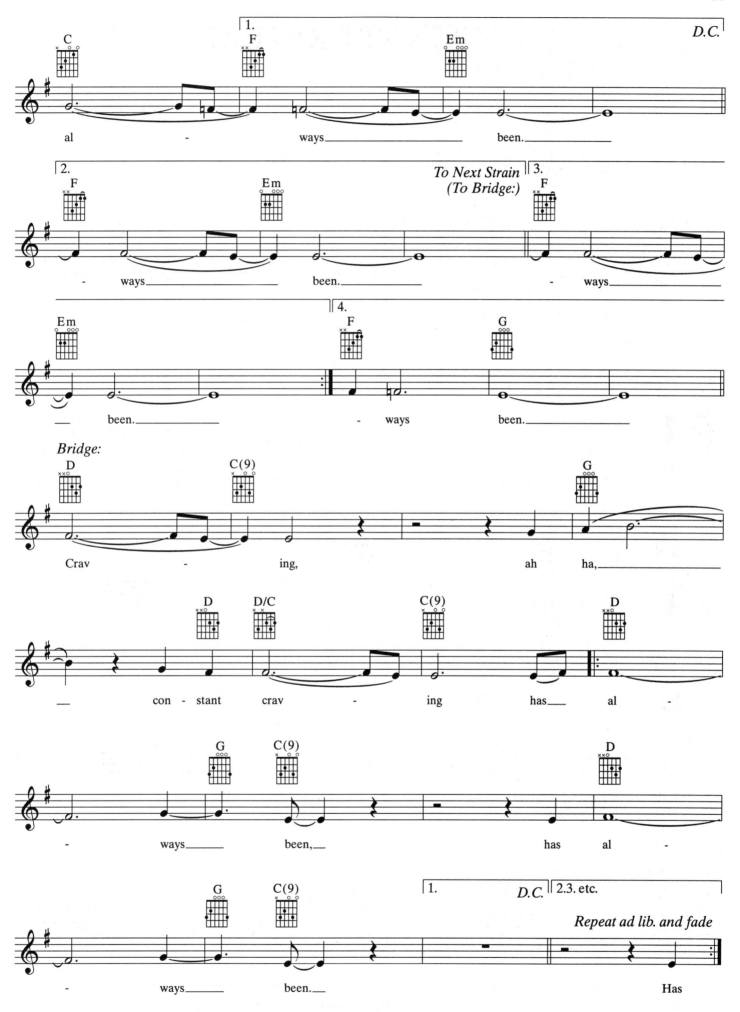

HOW DO I LIVE

Words and Music by
DIANE WARREN

Moderately slow ♩ = 92

1. How do I get through one night with-out you? If I had to live with-out you, what kind of life would that be? Oh, I, I need you in my arms, need you to hold. You're my world, my heart, my soul. If you ev-er leave, ba-by, you would take a-way ev-'ry-thing good in my life.

Verse:

2. *See additional lyrics*

Chorus:

And tell me now, how do I live with-out you? I want to know. How do I breathe with-out

How Do I Live - 2 - 1
GFM0001

© 1997 REALSONGS (ASCAP)
All Rights Reserved

Verse 2:
Without you, there'd be no sun in my sky,
There would be no love in my life,
There'd be no world left for me.
And I, baby, I don't know what I would do,
I'd be lost if I lost you.
If you ever leave,
Baby, you would take away everything real in my life.
And tell me now . . .
(To Chorus:)

DID I SHAVE MY LEGS FOR THIS?

Words and Music by
DEANA KAY CARTER and RHONDA HART

© 1996 Universal - PolyGram International Publishing, Inc.,
Door Number Two Music and Millermoo Music
All Rights for Door Number Two Music Controlled and Administered by
Universal - PolyGram International Publishing, Inc.
All Rights Reserved

Verse 2:
Now, when we first met, you promised we'd get
A house on a hill with a pool.
Well, this trailer stays wet and we're swimming in debt.
Now you want me to go back to school.
(To Chorus:)

CRYIN'

Words and Music by
STEVEN TYLER, JOE PERRY
and TAYLOR RHODES

© 1992 Universal - MCA Music Publishing, a Division of Universal Studios, Inc./
T. Rhodes Songs and EMI April Music Inc. / Swag Song Music, Inc.
All Rights for T. Rhodes Songs Controlled and Administered by
Universal - MCA Music Publishing, a Division of Universal Studios, Inc.
All Rights Reserved

DON'T SPEAK

Words and Music by
ERIC STEFANI and GWEN STEFANI

© 1995 Universal - MCA Music Publishing, Inc., A Division of Universal Studios, Inc.
and Knock Yourself Out Music
All Rights Administered by Universal - MCA Music Publishing, Inc., A Division of Universal Studios, Inc.
All Rights Reserved

Don't Speak - 3 - 1
GFM0001

EVERY MORNING

Words and Music by
SUGAR RAY, DAVID KAHNE, RICHARD BEAN,
PABLO TELLEZ and ABEL ZARATE

Gtr. tuned down 1/2 step:

⑥=E♭ ③=G♭
⑤=A♭ ②=B♭
④=D♭ ①=E♭

© 1999 WARNER-TAMERLANE PUBLISHING CORP., GRAVE LACK OF TALENT MUSIC,
JOSEPH "MCG" NICHOL, E EQUALS MUSIC and CANTERBURY MUSIC PUBLISHING
All Rights for GRAVE LACK OF TALENT MUSIC and JOSEPH "MCG" NICHOL
Administered by WARNER-TAMERLANE PUBLISHING CORP.
All Rights Reserved
"EVERY MORNING" contains samples from "SUAVECITO" by Richard Bean, Pablo Tellez and Abel Zarate
© Canterbury Music Publishing (BMI) Used by Permission

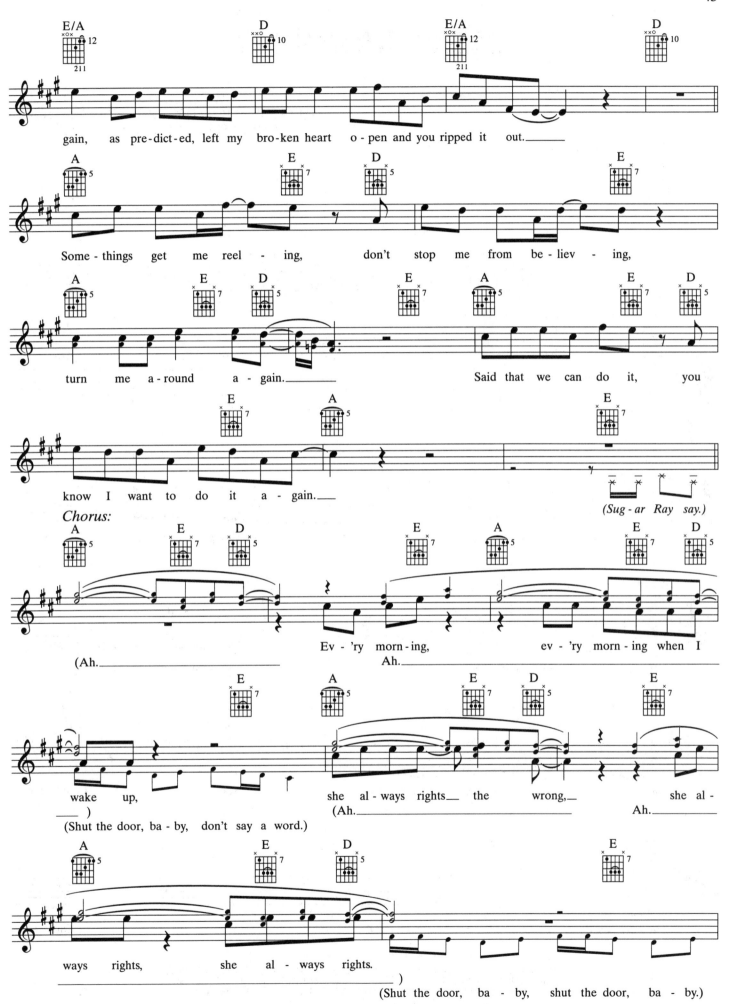

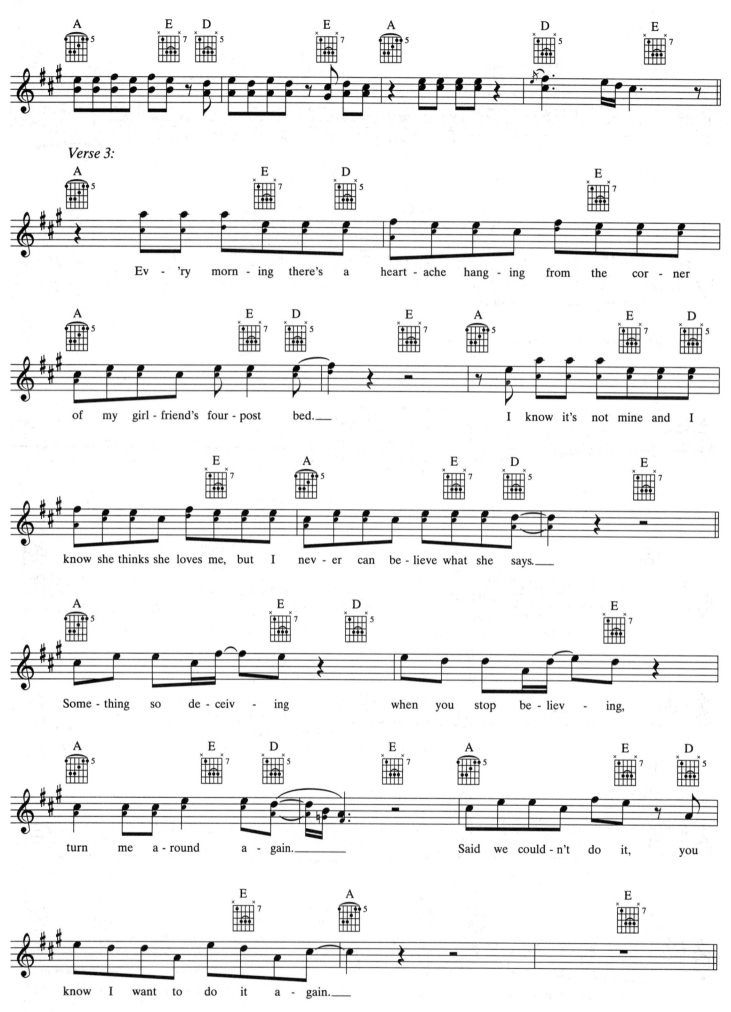

Verse 3:

Ev - 'ry morn - ing there's a heart - ache hang - ing from the cor - ner

of my girl - friend's four - post bed.___ I know it's not mine and I

know she thinks she loves me, but I nev - er can be - lieve what she says.___

Some - thing so de - ceiv - ing when you stop be - liev - ing,

turn me a - round a - gain.___ Said we could - n't do it, you

know I want to do it a - gain.___

48

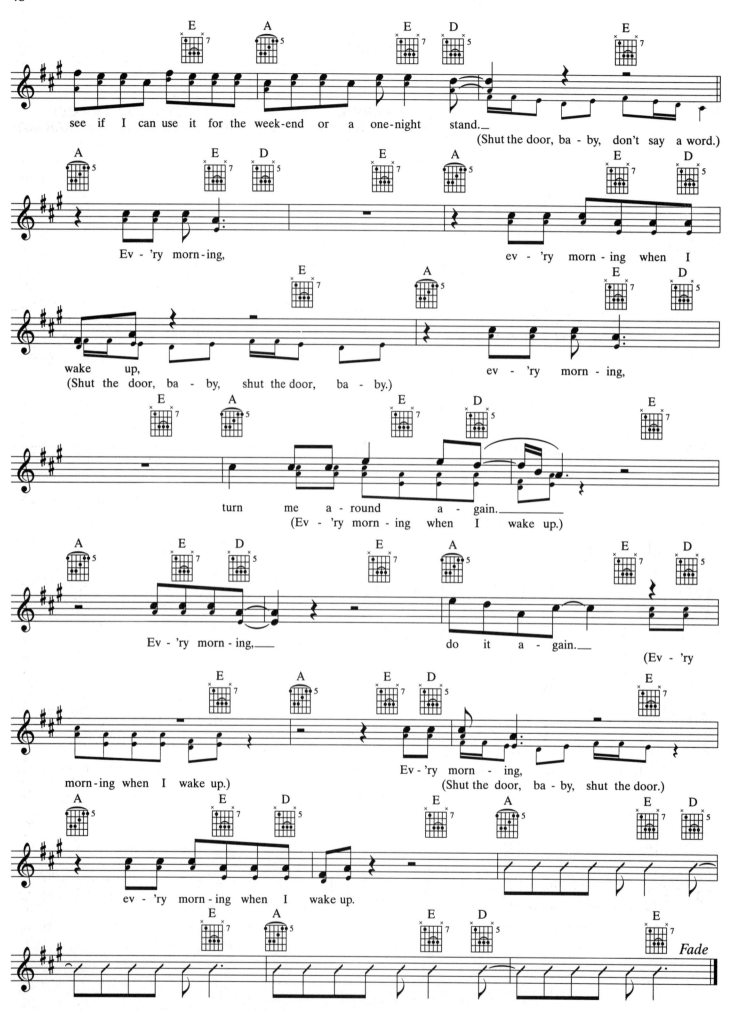

FLY

Words and Music by
MARK McGRATH, MURPHY KARGES, STAN FRAZIER,
RODNEY SHEPPARD, CRAIG BULLOCK and WILLIAM MARAGH

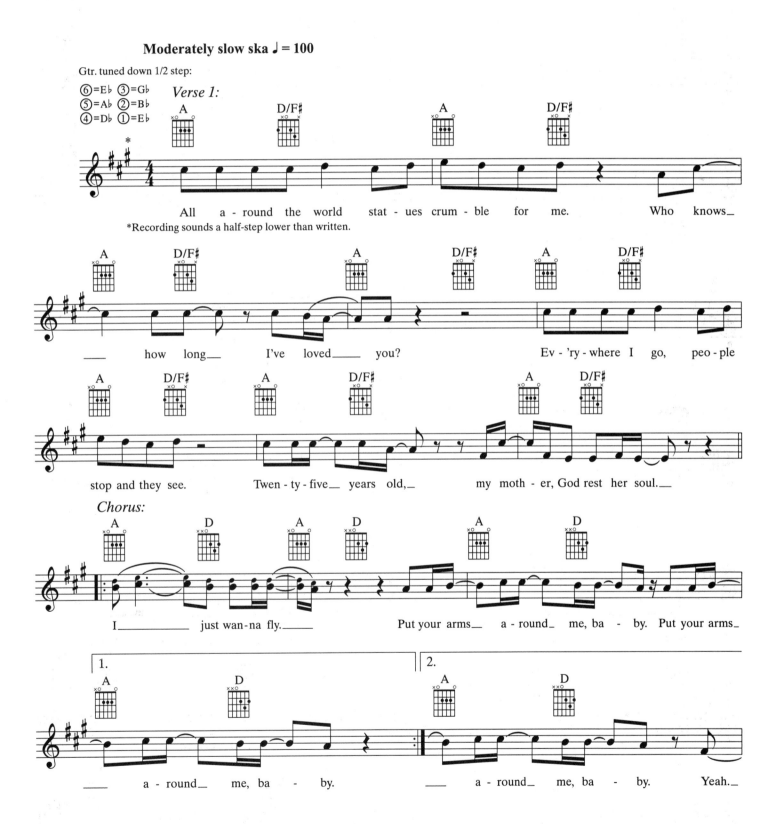

© 1997, 1998 WARNER-TAMERLANE PUBLISHING CORP., GRAVE LACK OF TALENT MUSIC,
ZOMBA ENTERPRISES, INC. and WILD APACHE MUSIC PUBLISHING, INC.
All Rights on behalf of GRAVE LACK OF TALENT MUSIC Administered by WARNER-TAMERLANE PUBLISHING CORP.
All Rights on behalf of WILD APACHE MUSIC PUBLISHING, INC. Administered by ZOMBA ENTERPRISES, INC.
All Rights Reserved

51

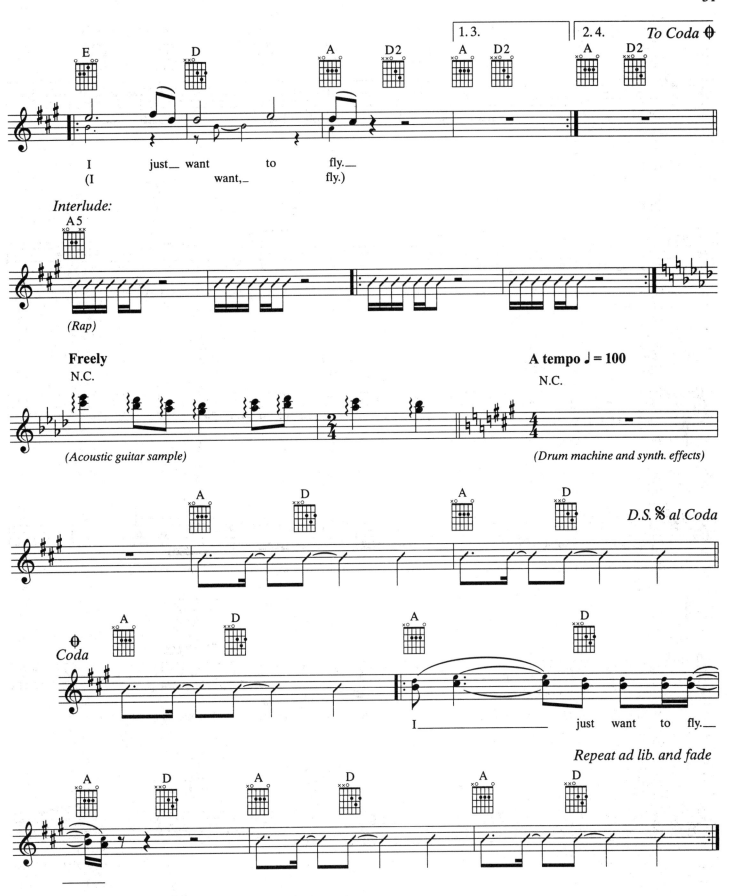

Verse 3:
All around the world statues crumble for me.
Who knows how long I've loved you?
Everyone I know has been so good to me.
Twenty-five years old,
My mother, God rest her soul.
(To Chorus:)

Fly - 3 - 3
GFM0001

FOOLISH GAMES

Words and Music by
JEWEL KILCHER

Moderately slow ♩ = 66

Verse:

1. You took your coat off and stood in the rain,
2. 3. 4. *See additional lyrics*

you're al - ways cra - zy like that.

And I watched from my win - dow,

al - ways felt I was out - side look - ing

1. 3. | 2. 4.

in on you.

Pre-chorus:

1. In case you failed to no - tice, in case you failed to see,
2. *See additional lyrics*

Foolish Games - 3 - 1
GFM0001

© 1995 WB MUSIC CORP. and WIGGLY TOOTH MUSIC
All Rights Administered by WB MUSIC CORP.
All Rights Reserved

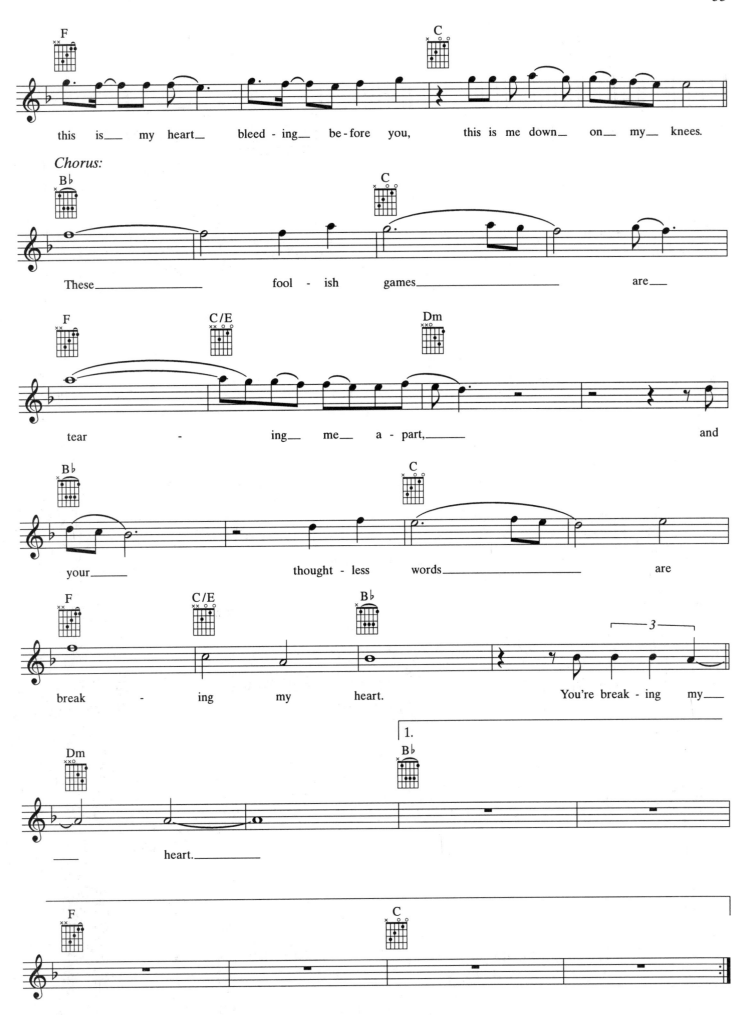

this is___ my heart___ bleed - ing___ be - fore you, this is me down___ on my___ knees.

Chorus:

These_____ fool - ish games_____ are___

tear - ing___ me a - part,_____ and

your_____ thought - less words_____ are

break - ing my heart. You're break - ing my___

1.

___ heart._____

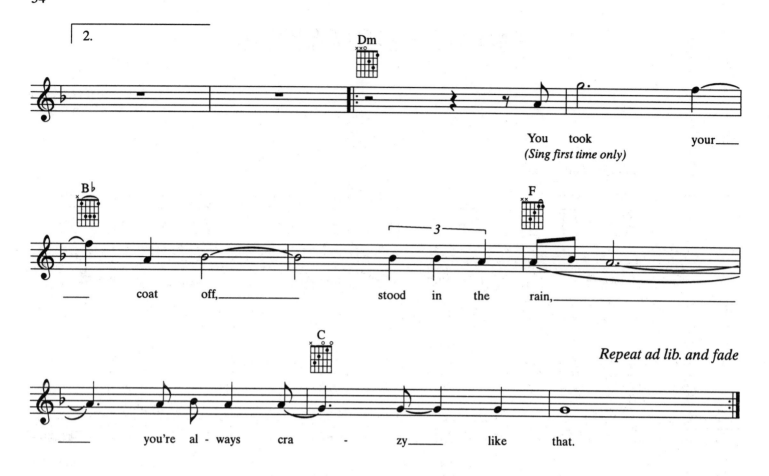

2.

Dm

You took your____

(Sing first time only)

B♭   F

____ coat off,____ stood in the rain,____

Repeat ad lib. and fade

C

____ you're al - ways cra - zy____ like that.

Verse 2:
You're always the mysterious one with
Dark eyes and careless hair,
You we're fashionably sensitive
But too cool to care.
You stood in my doorway with nothing to say
Besides some comment on the weather.
(To Pre-chorus 1:)

Verse 3:
You're always brilliant in the morning,
Smoking your cigarettes and talking over coffee.
Your philosophies on art, Baroque moved you.
You loved Mozart and you'd speak of your loved ones
As I clumsily strummed my guitar.

Verse 4:
You'd teach me of honest things,
Things that were daring, things that were clean.
Things that knew what an honest dollar did mean.
I hid my soiled hands behind my back.
Somewhere along the line, I must have gone
Off track with you.

Pre-chorus 2:
Excuse me, think I've mistaken you for somebody else,
Somebody who gave a damn, somebody more like myself.
(To Chorus:)

FROM A DISTANCE

Lyrics and Music by
JULIE GOLD

Slowly ♩ = 66

1. From a dis - tance, the world_ looks blue_ and green,_ and the
2.3. *See additional lyrics*

snow - capped_ moun - tains white. From a dis - tance, the o - cean meets_

_ the stream,_ and_ the ea - gle_ takes_ to_ flight. From_ a

dis - tance there_ is_ har - mo - ny,_ and it_ ech - oes through_ the land._

From a Distance - 3 - 1
GFM0001

© 1987 WING AND WHEEL MUSIC (BMI) and JULIE GOLD MUSIC (BMI)
All Rights on behalf of WING AND WHEEL MUSIC Administered by IRVING MUSIC, INC. (BMI)
All Rights Reserved

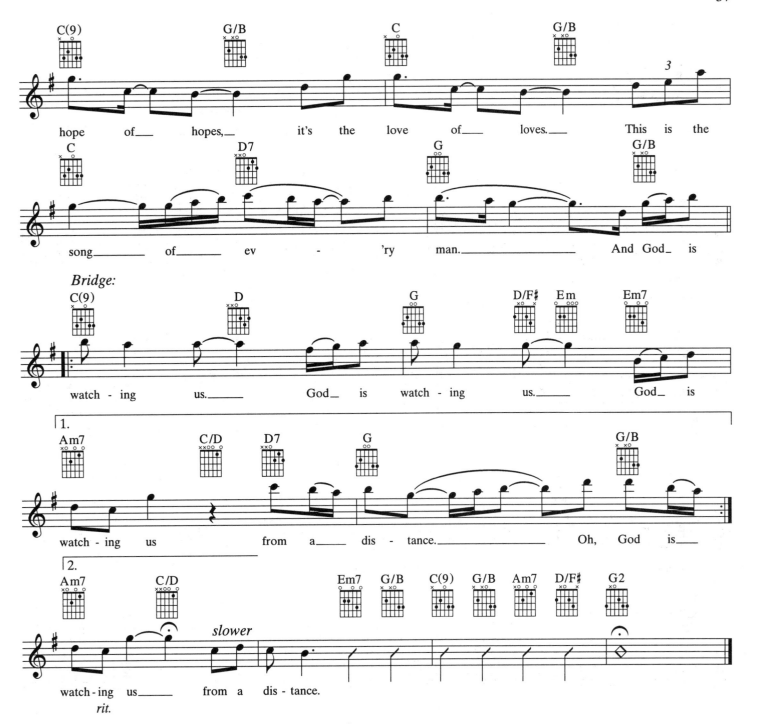

Verse 2:
From a distance, we all have enough,
And no one in need.
There are no guns, no bombs, no diseases,
No hungry mouths to feed.
From a distance, we are instruments
Marching in a common band;
Playing songs of hope, playing songs of peace,
They're the songs of every man.
(To Bridge:)

Verse 3:
From a distance, you look like my friend
Even though we are at war.
From a distance I just cannot comprehend
What all this fighting is for.
From a distance there is harmony
And it echoes through the land.
It's the hope of hopes, it's the love of loves.
It's the heart of every man.

HAND IN MY POCKET

Lyrics by
ALANIS MORISSETTE

Music by
ALANIS MORISSETTE and GLEN BALLARD

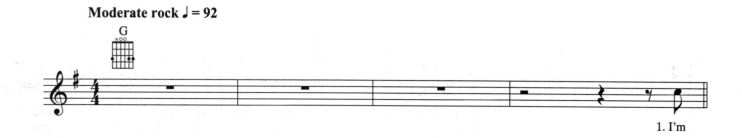

1. I'm

Verse:

broke but I'm_ hap - py,_____ I'm poor but I'm kind,____ I'm

2.3. *See additional lyrics*

short but I'm_ health - y, yeah.____ I'm_ high but I'm ground - ed,____ I'm

sane but I'm o - ver - whelmed, I'm lost but I'm hope - ful, ba -

Chorus:

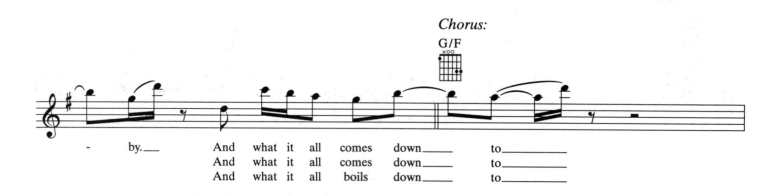

- by.____ And what it all comes down____ to_____
And what it all comes down____ to_____
And what it all boils down____ to_____

© 1995 Songs of Universal, Inc., Vanhurst Place, Universal - MCA Music Publishing,
A Division of Universal Studios, Inc. and Aerostation Corporation
All Rights for Vanhurst Place Controlled and Administered by Songs of Universal, Inc.
All Rights for Aerostation Corporation Controlled and Administered by
Universal - MCA Music Publishing, A Division of Universal Studios, Inc.
All Rights Reserved

Verse 2:
I feel drunk but I'm sober,
I'm young and I'm underpaid.
I'm tired but I'm workin', a-yeah.
I care but I'm restless,
I'm here but I'm really gone.
I'm wrong and I'm sorry, baby.
(To Chorus:)

Verse 3:
I'm free but I'm focused,
I'm green but I'm wise,
I'm hard but I'm friendly, baby.
I'm sad but I'm laughing,
I'm brave but I'm chicken-s***,
I'm sick but I'm pretty, ba-by.
(To Chorus:)

HANDS

Words and Music by
JEWEL KILCHER and PATRICK LEONARD

© 1998 WB MUSIC CORP., WIGGLY TOOTH MUSIC and BUMYAMAKI MUSIC
All Rights on behalf of WIGGLY TOOTH MUSIC Administered by WB MUSIC CORP.
All Rights on behalf of BUMYAMAKI MUSIC Administered by WIXEN MUSIC PUBLISHING, INC.
All Rights Reserved

Hands - 3 - 1
GFM0001

Verse 2:
Poverty stole your golden shoes,
It didn't steal your laughter.
And heartache came to visit me,
But I knew it wasn't ever after.
We'll fight not out of spite,
For someone must stand up for what's right.
'Cause where there's a man who has no voice,
There ours shall go on singing.
(To Chorus:)

GOOD RIDDANCE
(Time of Your Life)

Lyrics by
BILLIE JOE

Music by
BILLIE JOE and GREENDAY

Fast ♩ = 172

Verse:

1. An-oth-er turn-ing point,__ a fork__ stuck in__ the__ road.
2. So take the pho-to-graphs and still-frames__ in your__ mind.
3. (*Inst. solo ad lib.…*

Time grabs you by__ the__ wrist,__ di-rects__ __ you where__ to__ go.
Hang it on__ a__ shelf__ in good__ __ health and__ good__ time.

So make the best__ __ of__ this test__ and don't__ ask why.__
Tat-toos of mem-__ -o-ries and dead__ skin__ on trial.__

It's not a ques-__ -tion, but a les-son learned__ in__ time.
For what it's worth,__ __ it__ was worth__ all__ the__ while.
}
…end solo)

It's

© 1997 WB MUSIC CORP. and GREEN DAZE MUSIC
All Rights Administered by WB MUSIC CORP.
All Rights Reserved

HAVE I TOLD YOU LATELY

Words and Music by
VAN MORRISON

Moderately ♩ = 110

Chorus:

Have I told you late - ly_____ that I love you?_____

Have I told you there's no__ one a - bove you?__

Yeah, you fill my heart with glad - ness,__ take a - way my sad - ness.

Ease my trou - ble, that's what you do. 1. All I

Verse:

want is some of the Lord's glo - ry._____ He said

2. *(Inst. solo ad lib....*

Have I Told You Lately - 4 - 1
GFM0001

© 1989 Caledonia Publishing Ltd. and Exile Publishing Ltd.
All Rights Controlled and Administered by Universal - Songs of PolyGram International, Inc.
All Rights Reserved

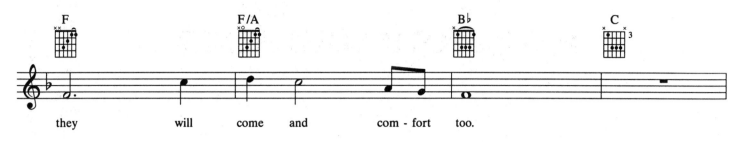

they will come and com - fort too.

Now you fill my life with laugh - ter, and you make it bet - ter.__

Ease my trou - bles, that's what you do.

. . . end solo)

Bridge:

Noth - ing else is so fine___ and it's yours and it's

mine_____ and it shines like the sun.

At the end of the day___ we shall give thanks and

Chorus:

way____ my sad - ness____ and   ease my

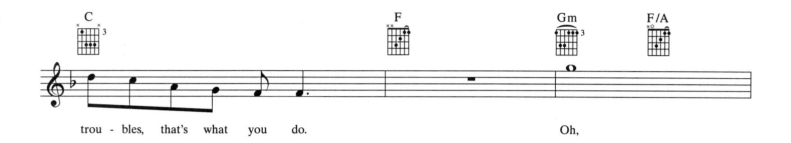

trou - bles, that's what you do.   Oh,

you fill my heart with glad - ness,_____ and   take a -

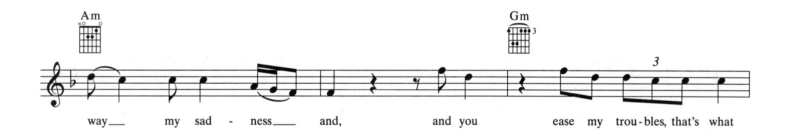

way____ my sad - ness____ and,   and you   ease my trou - bles, that's what

you, you,   you, you,   you, you, you, you, you, you, you, you,

you, you,   you,   you,   you,   you,   you.

Have I Told You Lately - 4 - 4
GFM0001

I CAN'T MAKE YOU LOVE ME

Lyrics and Music by
MIKE REID and ALLEN SHAMBLIN

I Can't Make You Love Me - 2 - 1
GFM0001

© 1991 ALMO MUSIC CORP./BRIO BLUES MUSIC/HAYES STREET MUSIC, INC. (ASCAP)
All Rights Administered by ALMO MUSIC CORP.
All Rights Reserved

I'LL BE THERE FOR YOU

Words by
DAVID CRANE, MARTA KAUFFMAN, ALLEE WILLIS,
PHIL SOLEM and DANNY WILDE

Music by
MICHAEL SKLOFF

1. So no____ one told____ you life____ was
2. You're still____ in bed____ at ten____ and

gon - na be____ this way.____ Your job's____ a joke,____
work be - gan____ at eight.____ You've burned____ your break -

____ you're broke,____ your love life's D. O. A.____
- fast, so far, things are go - ing great.____

(1.3.) It's like____ you're al - ways stuck____ in sec - ond gear.____
(2.) Your moth - er warned_ you there'd_ be days like these.____

Well, it has - n't been____ your day,____ your week,_ your month,
But she did - n't tell____ you when____ the world_ has

I'll Be There for You - 3 - 1
GFM0001
© 1994 WB MUSIC CORP. and WARNER-TAMERLANE PUBLISHING CORP.
All Rights Reserved

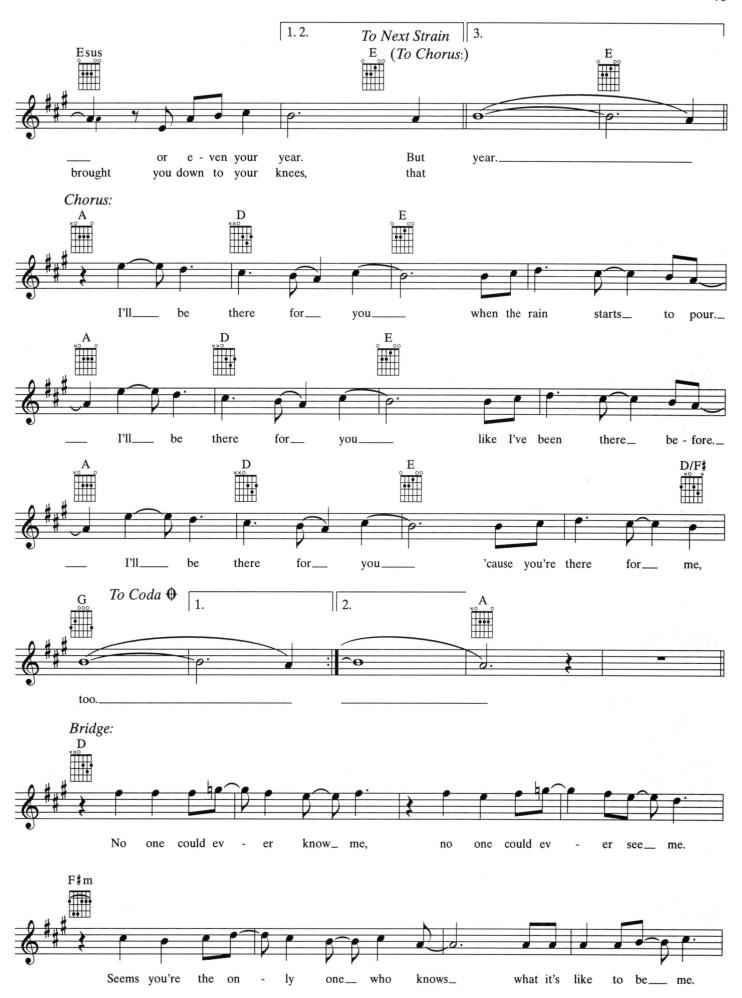

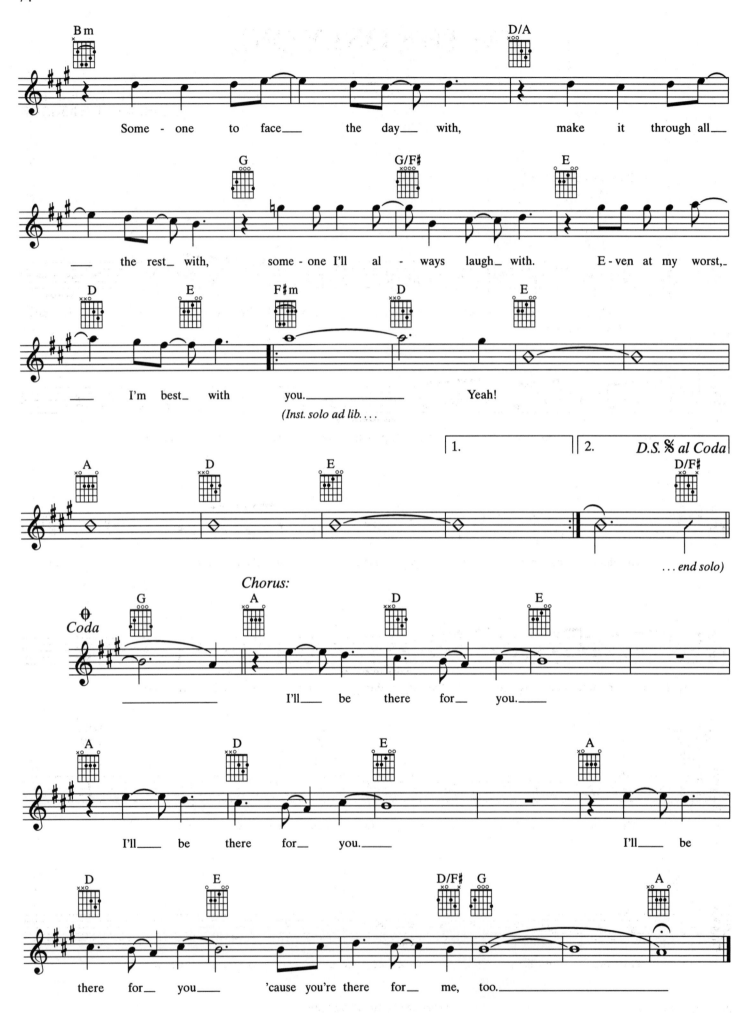

I'M THE ONLY ONE

Words and Music by
MELISSA ETHERIDGE

Moderately ♩ = 84

Verse:

1. Please, ba - by, can't you see my mind's a burn - ing hell?__ I got

2. *See additional lyrics*

ra - zors a - rip - pin' and tear - in' and strip - pin' my heart a - part as well.

To - night you told me that you ache for some - thing new.__ And

some oth - er wom - an is look - in' like some - thing that might be good for you.

Go on and hold her 'til the scream - ing is gone.__

Go on, be - lieve her when she tells you noth - ing's wrong.__

© 1993 M.L.E. MUSIC (ASCAP)
All Rights Administered by ALMO MUSIC CORP. (ASCAP)
All Rights Reserved

Repeat ad lib. and fade

Verse 2:
Please, baby, can't you see I'm trying to explain?
I've been here before and I'm locking the door,
And I'm not going back again.
Her eyes and arms and skin won't make it go away.
You'll wake up tomorrow and wrestle the sorrow
That holds you down today.
(To Chorus:)

JUST A GIRL

Words and Music by
ERIC STEFANI and GWEN STEFANI

© 1995 Universal - MCA Music Publishing, Inc., A Division of Universal Studios, Inc.
and Knock Yourself Out Music
All Rights Administered by Universal - MCA Music Publishing, Inc., A Division of Universal Studios, Inc.
All Rights Reserved

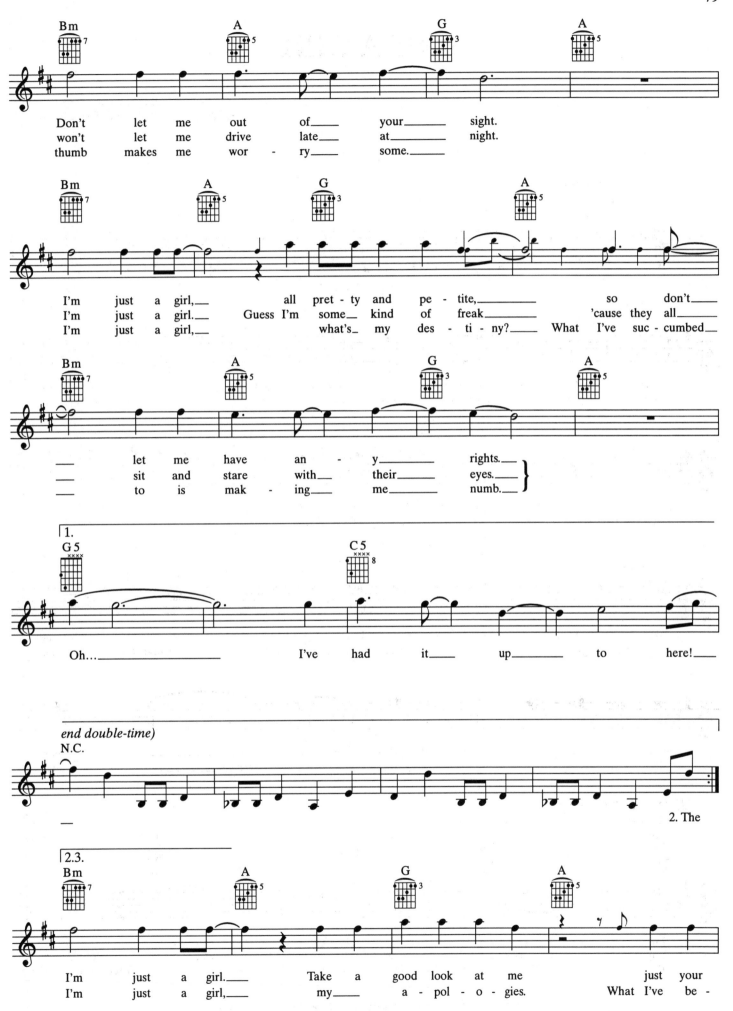

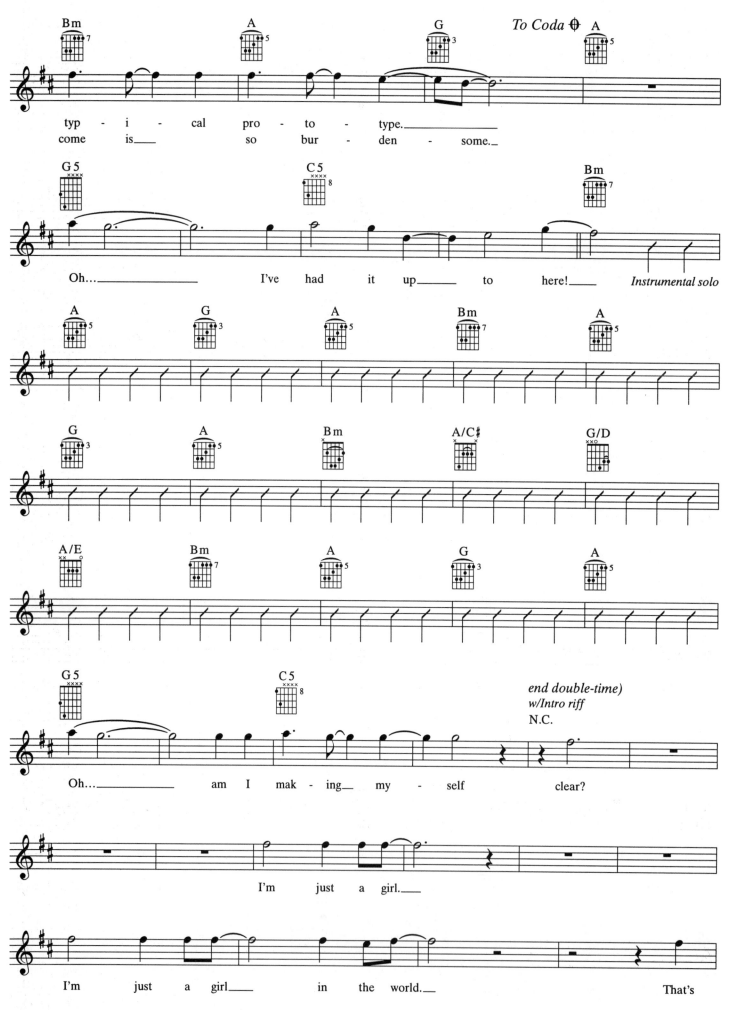

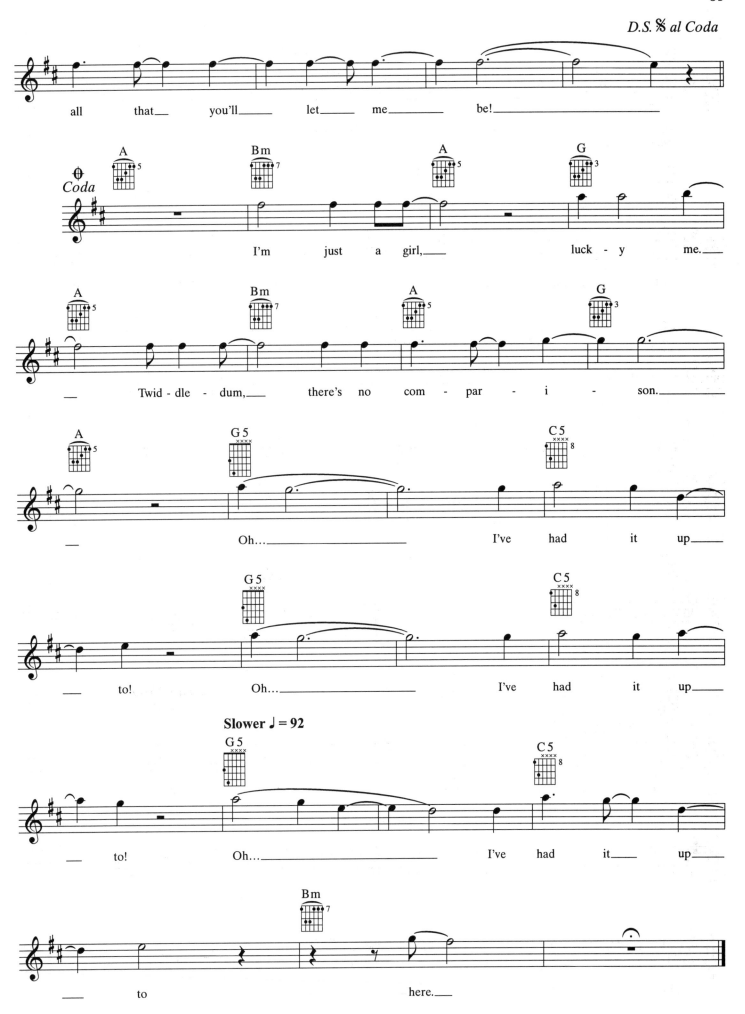

KISS FROM A ROSE

Words and Music by
SEAL

© 1994 PERFECT SONGS LIMITED, 42-46 St. Luke's Mews, London W11
All Rights Reserved

IRONIC

Lyrics by
ALANIS MORISSETTE

Music by
ALANIS MORISSETTE and GLEN BALLARD

© 1995 Songs of Universal, Inc., Vanhurst Place, Universal - MCA Music Publishing,
A Division of Universal Studios, Inc. and Aerostation Corporation
All Rights for Vanhurst Place Controlled and Administered by Songs of Universal, Inc.
All Rights for Aerostation Corporation Controlled and Administered by
Universal - MCA Music Publishing, A Division of Universal Studios, Inc.
All Rights Reserved

Verse 2:
Mister Play It Safe was afraid to fly.
He packed his suitcase and kissed his kids goodbye.
He waited his whole damn life to take that flight.
And as the plane crashed down he thought, "Well isn't this nice?"
And isn't it ironic? Don't cha think?
(To Chorus:)

LIVIN' LA VIDA LOCA

Words and Music by
ROBI ROSA and DESMOND CHILD

© 1999 A Phantom Vox Publishing,
Universal - PolyGram International Publishing, Inc. and Desmophobia
All Rights for A Phantom Vox Publishing Administered by Warner-Tamerlane Publishing Corp.
All Rights Reserved

Livin' la Vida Loca - 3 - 1
GFM0001

Verse 3:
Woke up in New York City
In a funky, cheap hotel.
She took my heart and she took my money.
She must have slipped me a sleeping pill.

Bridge 2:
She never drinks the water
And makes you order French champagne.
Once you've had a taste of her,
You'll never be the same.
Yeah, she'll make you go insane.
(To Chorus:)

LIVIN' ON THE EDGE

Words and Music by
STEVEN TYLER, JOE PERRY
and MARK HUDSON

© 1992 Universal - MCA Music Publishing, a Division of Universal Studios, Inc./
Beef Puppet Music and EMI April Music Inc. / Swag Song Music, Inc.
All Rights for Beef Puppet Music Controlled and Administered by
Universal - MCA Music Publishing, a Division of Universal Studios, Inc.
All Rights Reserved

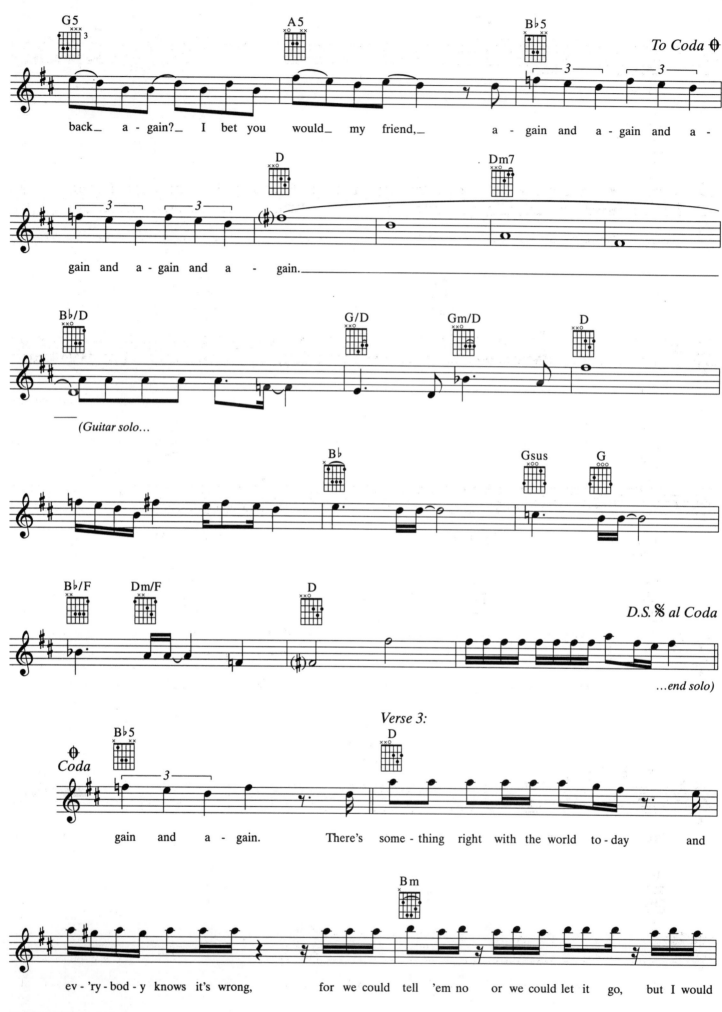

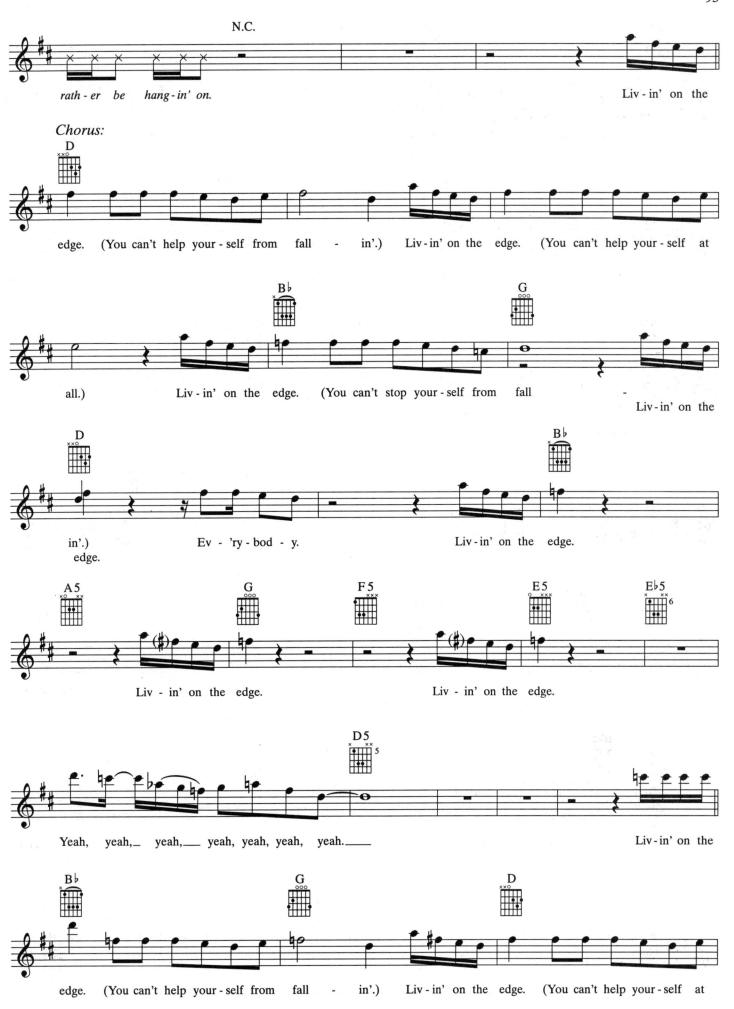

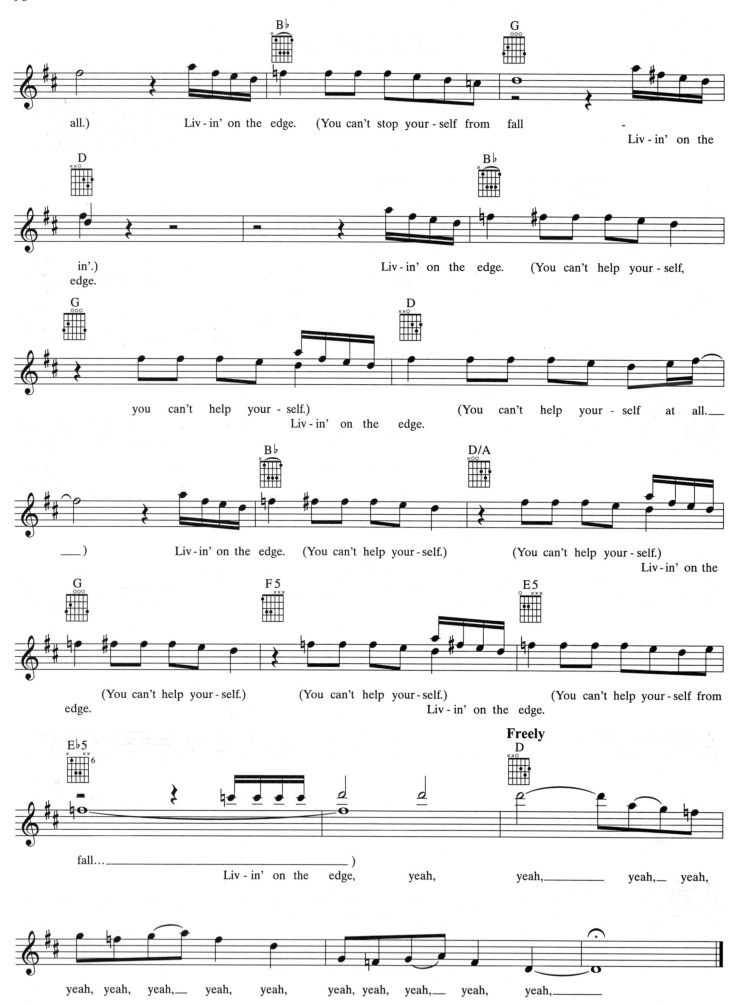

LONGVIEW

Words and Music by
**BILLIE JOE ARMSTRONG,
FRANK WRIGHT** and
MICHAEL PRITCHARD

Longview - 3 - 1
GFM0001

© 1994 WB MUSIC CORP. and GREEN DAZE MUSIC
All Rights Administered by WB MUSIC CORP.
All Rights Reserved

98

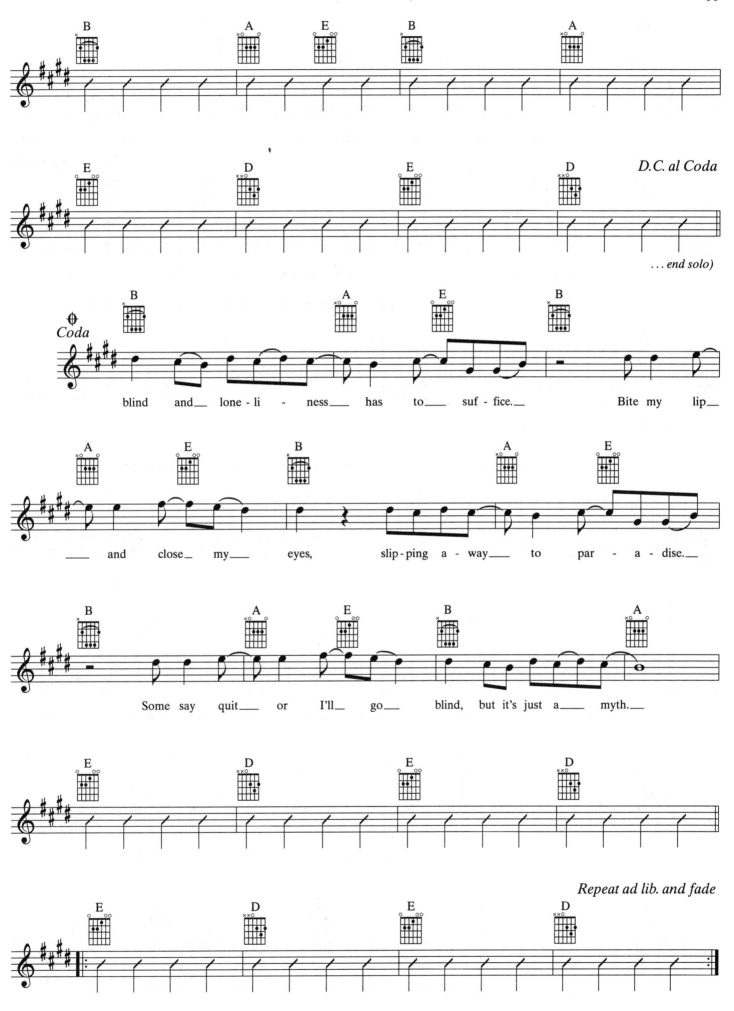

MMMBOP

Words and Music by
ISAAC HANSON, TAYLOR HANSON
and ZAC HANSON

© 1997 JAM 'N' BREAD MUSIC (ASCAP)
All Rights Administered by HEAVY HARMONY MUSIC
All Rights Reserved

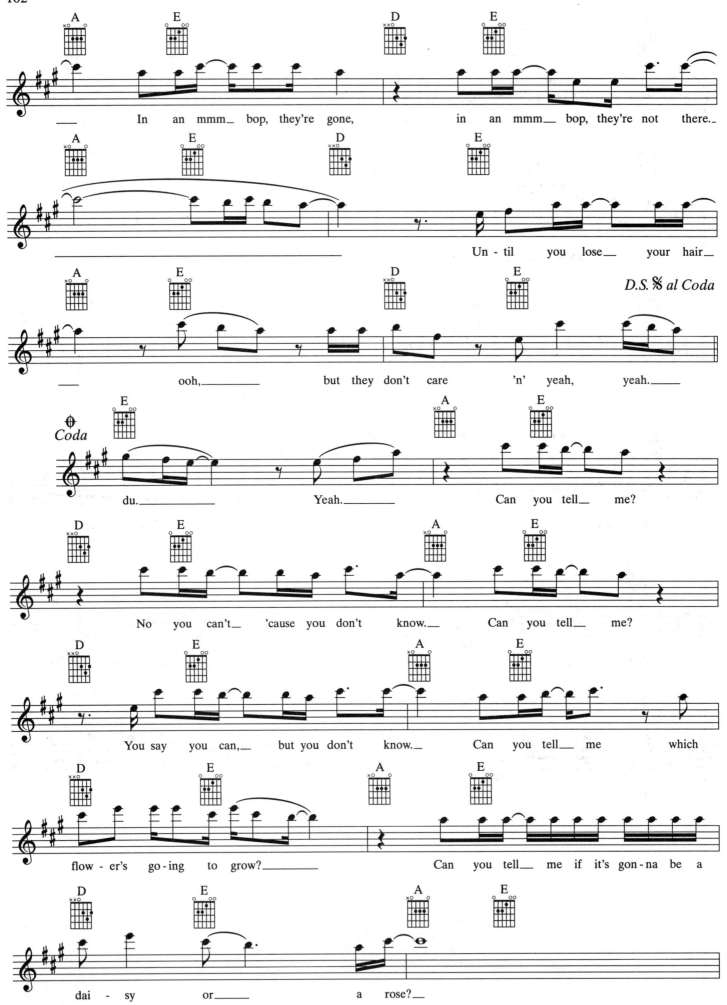

Verse 3:
Plant a seed, plant a flower, plant a rose.
You can plant any one of those.
Keep planting to find out which one grows.
It's a secret no one knows.
It's a secret no one knows.
Oh, no one knows.
(To Chorus:)

ONE HEADLIGHT

Words and Music by
JAKOB DYLAN

Moderately ♩ = 96

Verses 1 & 2:

1. So long a-go, I don't re-mem-ber when,__ that's when they said I lost__ my on-ly
2. *See additional lyrics*

friend. Well, they said she died eas-y of a bro-ken-heart dis-ease, as I

lis-tened through the cem-e-ter-y trees.

2. I seen the

Chorus:

Hey,_____ come on, try a lit-tle, noth-in' is for-ev-er.

One Headlight - 4 - 1
GFM0001

© 1996 WB MUSIC CORP. and BROTHER JUMBO MUSIC
All Rights Administered by WB MUSIC CORP.
All Rights Reserved

106

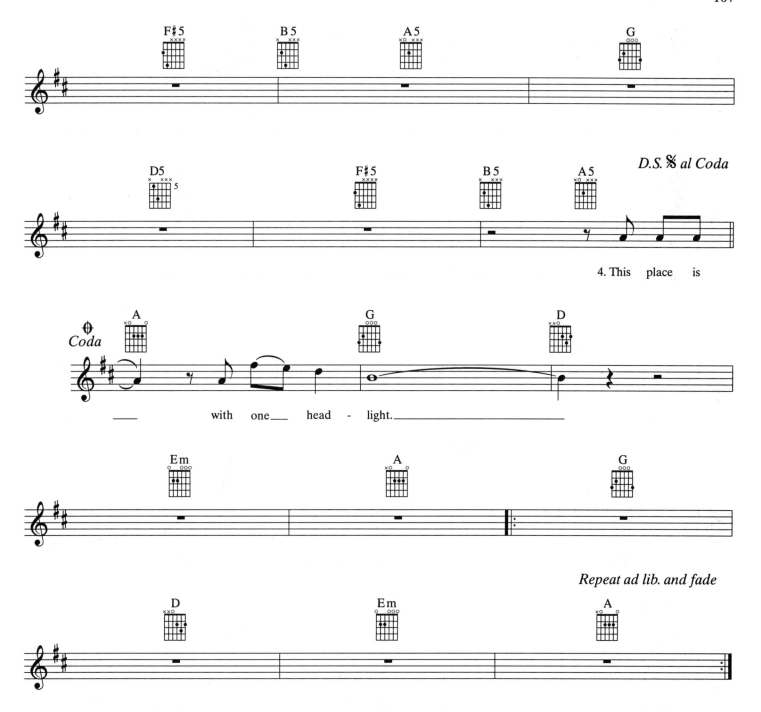

Verse 2:
I seen the sun comin' up at the funeral at dawn,
Of the long broken arm of human law.
Now, it always seemed such a waste,
She always had a pretty face.
I wonder why she hung around this place.
(To Chorus:)

Verse 4:
This place is old, and it feels just like a beat-up truck.
I turn the engine, but the engine doesn't turn.
It smells of cheap wine and cigarettes,
This place is always such a mess.
Sometimes I think I'd like to watch it burn.
Now, I sit alone, and I feel just like somebody else.
Man, I ain't changed, but I know I ain't the same.
But somewhere here, in between these city walls of dying dreams,
I think her death, it must be killing me.
(To Chorus:)

ONE OF US

Words and Music by
ERIC BAZILIAN

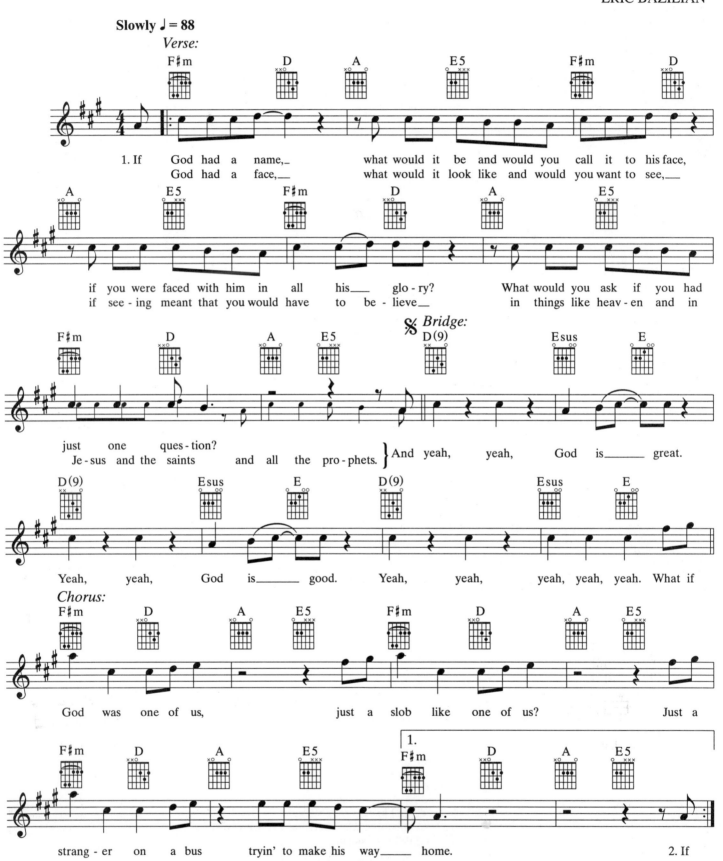

1. If God had a name,___ what would it be and would you call it to his face,
God had a face,___ what would it look like and would you want to see,___

if you were faced with him in all his___ glo - ry? What would you ask if you had
if see - ing meant that you would have to be - lieve___ in things like heav - en and in

just one ques - tion?
Je - sus and the saints and all the pro - phets.} And yeah, yeah, God is___ great.

Yeah, yeah, God is___ good. Yeah, yeah, yeah, yeah, yeah. What if

Chorus:
God was one of us, just a slob like one of us? Just a

strang - er on a bus tryin' to make his way___ home.   2. If

One of Us - 2 - 1
GFM0001

© 1995, 1996 HUMAN BOY MUSIC (ASCAP)
All Rights Administered by WB MUSIC CORP.
All Rights Reserved

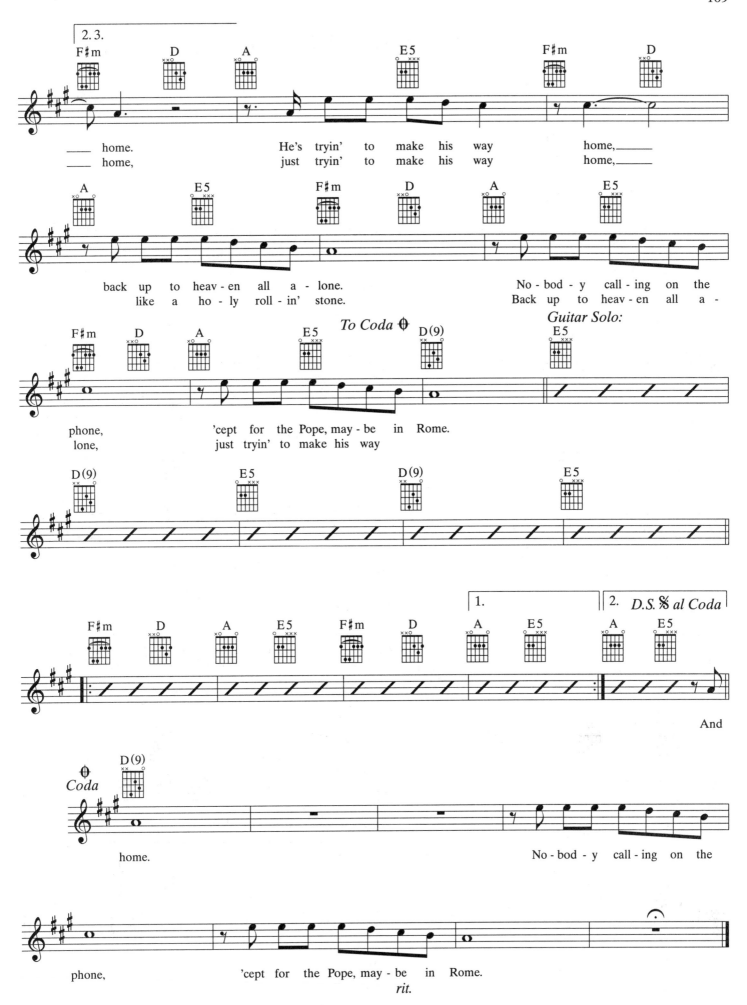

MORE THAN WORDS

Lyrics and Music by
BETTENCOURT, CHERONE

*Recording sounds a half-step lower than written.

© 1990 FUNKY METAL PUBLISHING (ASCAP)
All Rights Administered by ALMO MUSIC CORP. (ASCAP)
All Rights Reserved

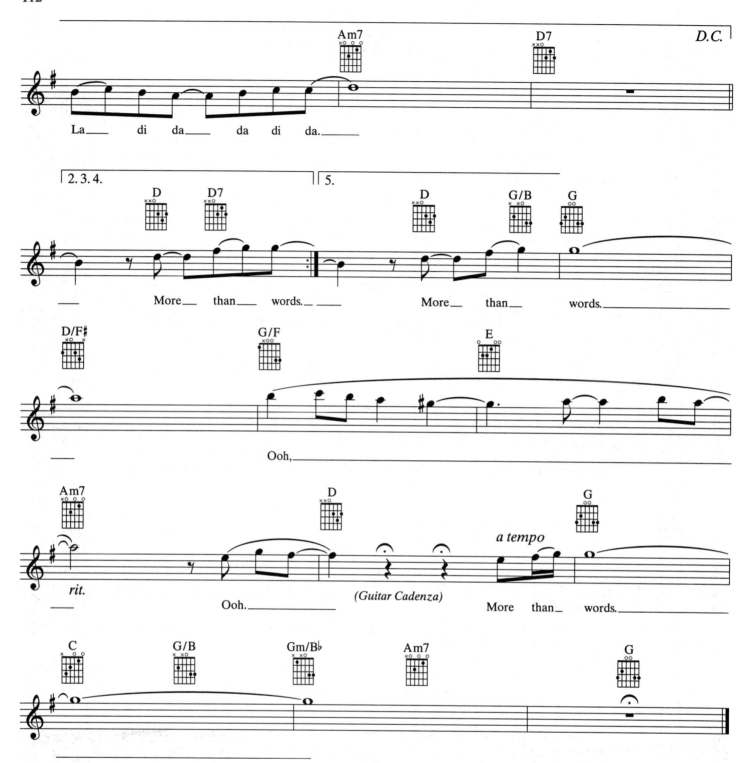

Verse 2:
Now that I have tried to talk to you
And make you understand,
All you have to do is close your eyes
And just reach out your hands.
And touch me, hold me close, don't ever let me go.
More than words is all I ever needed you to show.
Then you wouldn't have to say
That you love me 'cause I'd already know.
(To Chorus:)

ONE WEEK

Words and Music by
ED ROBERTSON

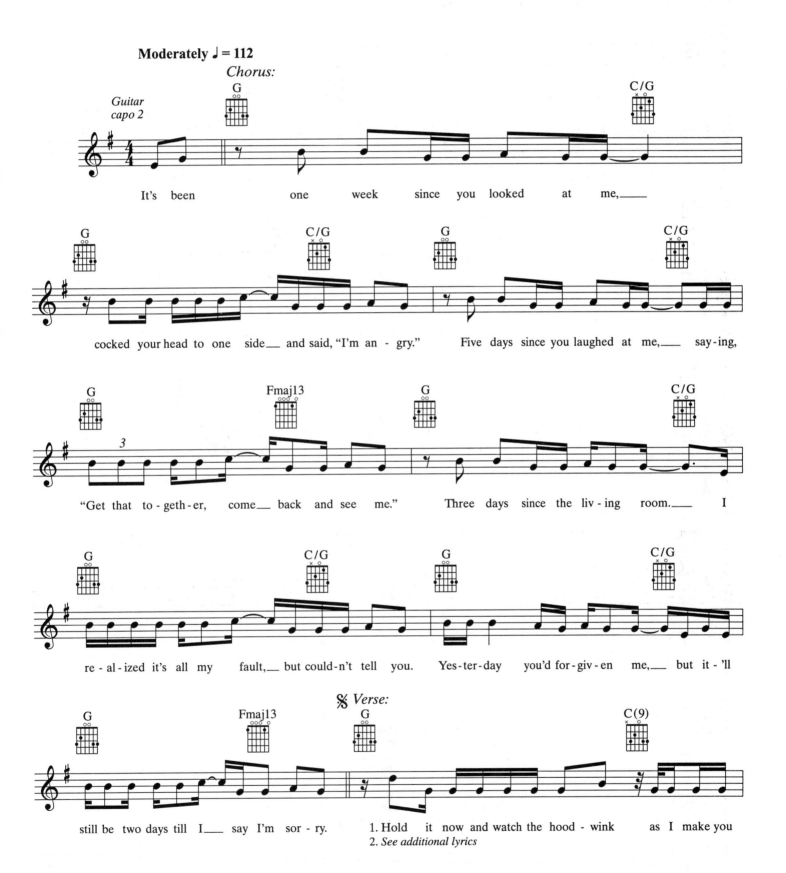

© 1998 WB MUSIC CORP. and TREAT BAKER MUSIC
All Rights Administered by WB MUSIC CORP.
All Rights Reserved

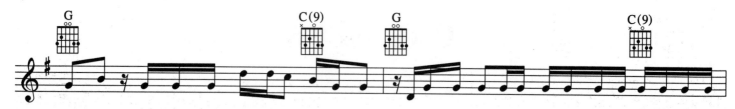

stop, think. You'll think you're look-ing at Aq-ua-man.   I sum-mon fish to the dish, al-though I like the Cha-let

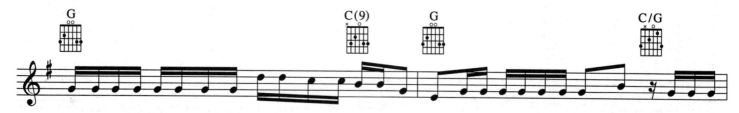

Swiss, I like the su-shi 'cause it's nev-er touched a fry-ing pan. Hot like wa-sa-be when I bust rhymes,   big like Le-

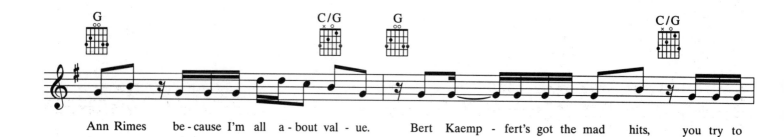

Ann Rimes   be-cause I'm all a-bout val-ue.   Bert Kaemp-fert's got the mad   hits,   you try to

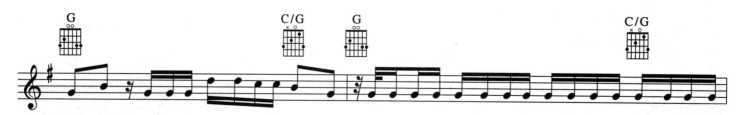

match wits,   you try to hold me, but I bust through. Gon-na make a break and take a fake. I'd like a stink-in', ach-in'

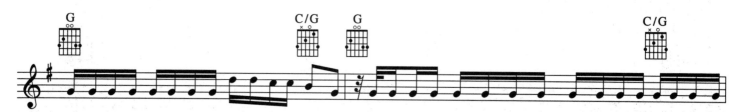

shake. I like va-nil-la, it's the fin-est of the fla-vors.   Got-ta see the show,'cause then you'll know the ver-ti-go is gon-na

Bridge:

grow,'cause it's so dan-ger-ous, you'll have to sign a waiv-er. 1. How can I help it if I think you're fun-ny when you're mad?
                                                                  2. *See additional lyrics*

116

sit back   and wait till   you__ say you're   sor - ry.

still be   two days till   we__ say we're   sor - ry.

It - 'll

It - 'll

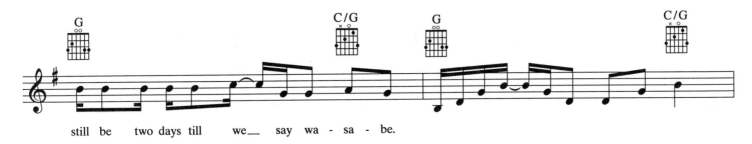

still be two days till we— say wa - sa - be.

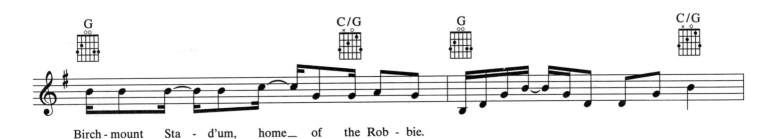

Birch - mount Sta - d'um, home— of the Rob - bie.

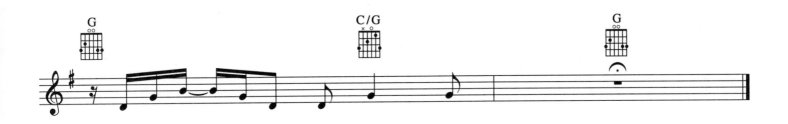

Verse 2:
Chickity China the Chinese chicken,
Have a drumstick and your brain stops tickin'.
Watchin' X-Files with no lights on.
We're dans la maison.
I hope the Smoking Man's in this one.
Like Harrison Ford, I'm getting frantic.
Like Sting, I tantric.
Like Snickers, guaranteed to satisfy.
Like Kurasawa, I made mad films.
OK, I don't make films,
But if I did, they'd have a Samurai.
Gonna get a set a better clubs.
Gonna find the kind with tiny nubs.
Just so my irons aren't always flying
Off the back-swing.
Gotta get in tune with Sailor Moon,
'Cause the cartoon has got
The boom Anime babes
That make me think the wrong thing.

Bridge 2:
How can I help it if I think you're funny
When you're mad?
Tryin' hard not to smile though I feel bad.
I'm the kind of guy who laughs at a funeral.
Can't understand what I mean?
Well, you soon will.
I have a tendency to wear
My mind on my sleeve.
I have a history of taking off my shirt.

Chorus 3:
It's been one week since you looked at me,
Dropped your arms to your sides
And said, "I'm sorry."
Five days since I laughed at you and said,
"You just did just what I thought
You were gonna do."
Three days since the living room.
We realized we're both to blame,
But what could we do?
Yesterday you just smiled at me
'Cause it'll still be two days
Till we say we're sorry.

ONLY HAPPY WHEN IT RAINS

Words and Music by
BUTCH VIG, DOUG ERICKSON,
STEVE MARKER and SHIRLEY MANSON

Only Happy When It Rains - 3 - 1
GFM0001

© 1995 IRVING MUSIC, INC. and VIBECRUSHER MUSIC (BMI) and DEADARM MUSIC (ASCAP)
All Rights Reserved

120

PRETENDING

Words and Music by
JERRY LYNN WILLIAMS

Moderately ♩ = 120

Verses 1 & 4:

1. How man-y times___ must we tell the tale?___ How man-y times___ must we fail?___
4. *(Inst. solo ad lib. . . .*

___ Liv - ing in a lost___ mem - o - ry___ you just re - called.___

Verses 2, 3, & 5:

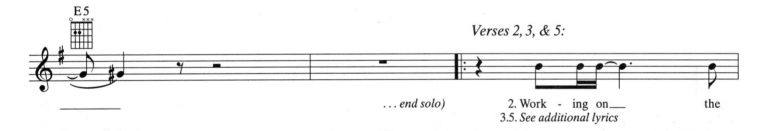

. . . *end solo)* 2. Work - ing on___ the
3.5. *See additional lyrics*

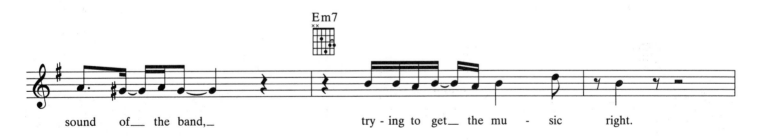

sound of___ the band,___ try - ing to get___ the mu - sic right.

To Coda ⊕

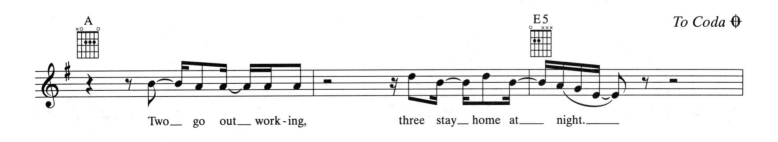

Two___ go out___ work - ing, three stay___ home at___ night.___

Pretending - 3 - 1
GFM0001

© 1985, 1990 Universal - Songs of PolyGram International,
Careers - BMG Music Publishing, Inc. and Red Brazos Music, Inc.
All Rights Reserved

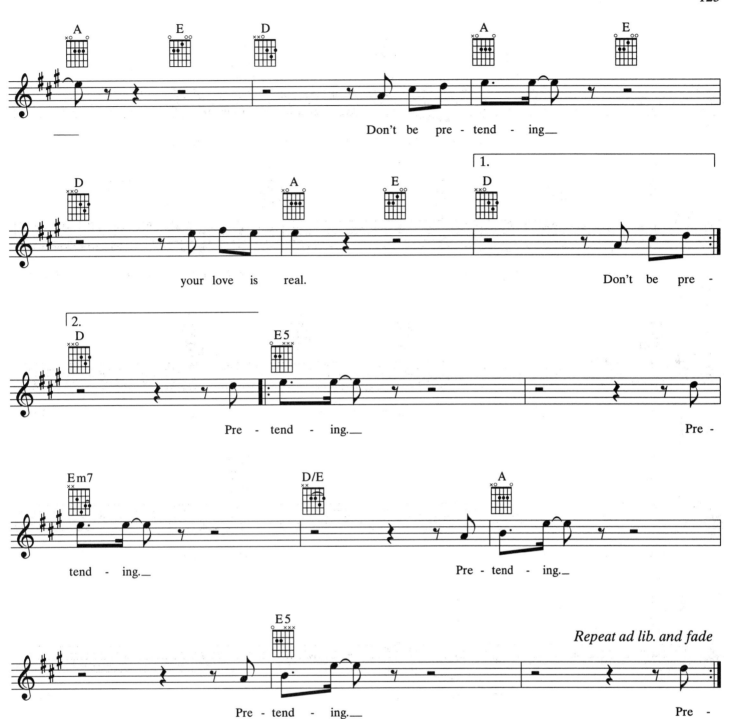

Don't be pre - tend - ing__

1.

your love is real.   Don't be pre -

2.

Pre - tend - ing.__   Pre -

tend - ing.__   Pre - tend - ing.__

Repeat ad lib. and fade

Pre - tend - ing.__   Pre -

Verse 3:
Satisfied but lost in love,
Situations change.
You're never who you used to think you are,
How strange.
(To Chorus:)

Verse 5:
I get lost in alibis,
Sadness can't prevail,
Everybody knows strong love
Can't fail.
(To Chorus:)

RAG DOLL

Words and Music by STEVEN TYLER, JOE PERRY,
JIM VALLANCE and HOLLY KNIGHT

Moderate rock shuffle ♩ = 80

© 1987 AERO DYNAMICS MUSIC PUBLISHING, INC. (BMI)/CALYPSO TOONZ (PRS)/
IRVING MUSIC, INC. (BMI)/THE MAKIKI PUBLISHING CO., LTD./
COLGEMS-EMI MUSIC INC./KNIGHTY-KNIGHT MUSIC
All Rights Reserved

126

SAVE TONIGHT

Words and Music by
EAGLE-EYE CHERRY

© 1998 DIESEL 2 PUBLISHING and MANAGEMENT AB
All Rights Administered by WARNER-TAMERLANE PUBLISHING CORP.
All Rights Reserved

130

Guitar solo ad lib.

Repeat ad lib. and fade

Verse 2:
There's a log on the fire
And it burns like me for you,
Tomorrow comes with one desire,
To take me away, oh it's true.
It ain't easy to say goodbye,
Darling, please don't start to cry,
'Cause, girl, you know I've got to go
And, Lord, I wish it wasn't so.
(To Chorus:)

SOMEDAY

Words and Music by
SUGAR RAY and DAVID KAHNE

© 1999 WARNER-TAMERLANE PUBLISHING CORP.,
GRAVE LACK OF TALENT MUSIC, JOSEPH "MCG" NICHOL and E EQUALS MUSIC
All Rights for GRAVE LACK OF TALENT MUSIC and JOSEPH "MCG" NICHOL
Administered by WARNER-TAMERLANE PUBLISHING CORP.
All Rights Reserved

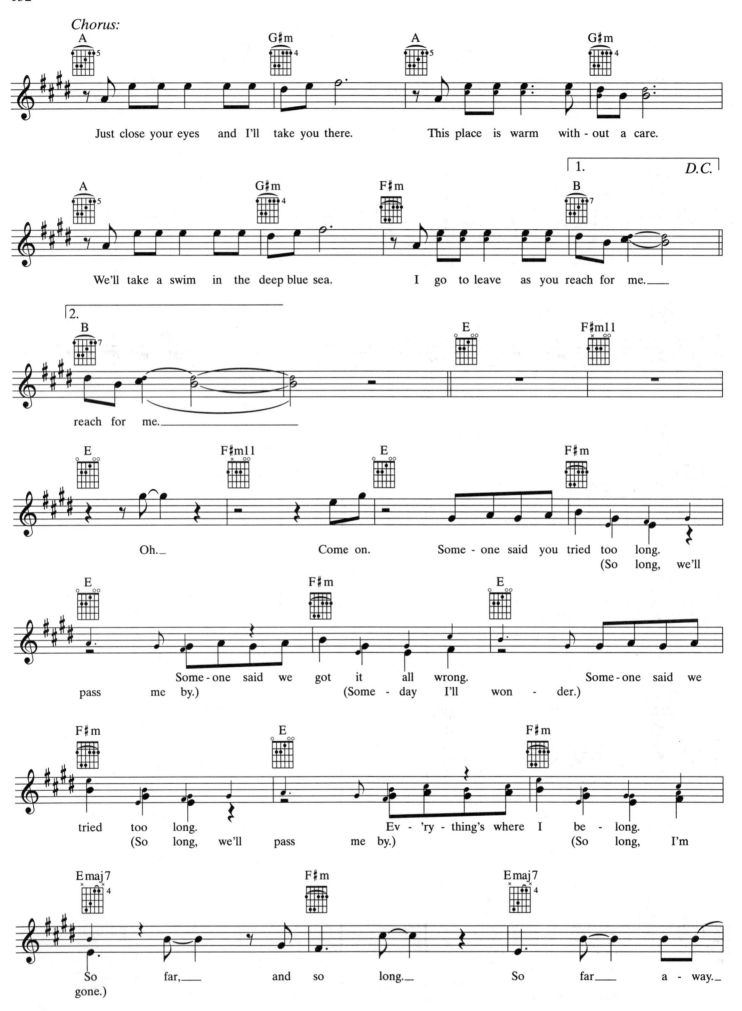

SPIDERWEBS

Words and Music by
ERIC STEFANI and GWEN STEFANI

© 1995 Universal - MCA Music Publishing, Inc., A Division of Universal Studios, Inc.
and Knock Yourself Out Music
All Rights Administered by Universal - MCA Music Publishing, Inc., A Division of Universal Studios, Inc.
All Rights Reserved

My dreams be - come night - mares_____

D.S. % al Coda

'cause you're ring - ing____ in my ears.____

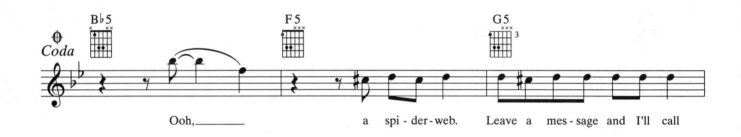

Coda

Ooh,____ a spi - der - web. Leave a mes - sage and I'll call

you back. I'm walk - ing in - to spi - der - webs, so,

leave a mes - sage and I'll call you back. It's all your__

__ fault.__ I screen my phone calls.__ No mat - ter, mat - ter, mat - ter

SUNNY CAME HOME

Words and Music by
SHAWN COLVIN and JOHN LEVENTHAL

© 1996 WB MUSIC CORP. (ASCAP), SCRED SONGS (ASCAP) and LEV-A-TUNES (ASCAP)
All Rights on behalf of SCRED SONGS (ASCAP) Administered by WB MUSIC CORP. (ASCAP)
All Rights Reserved

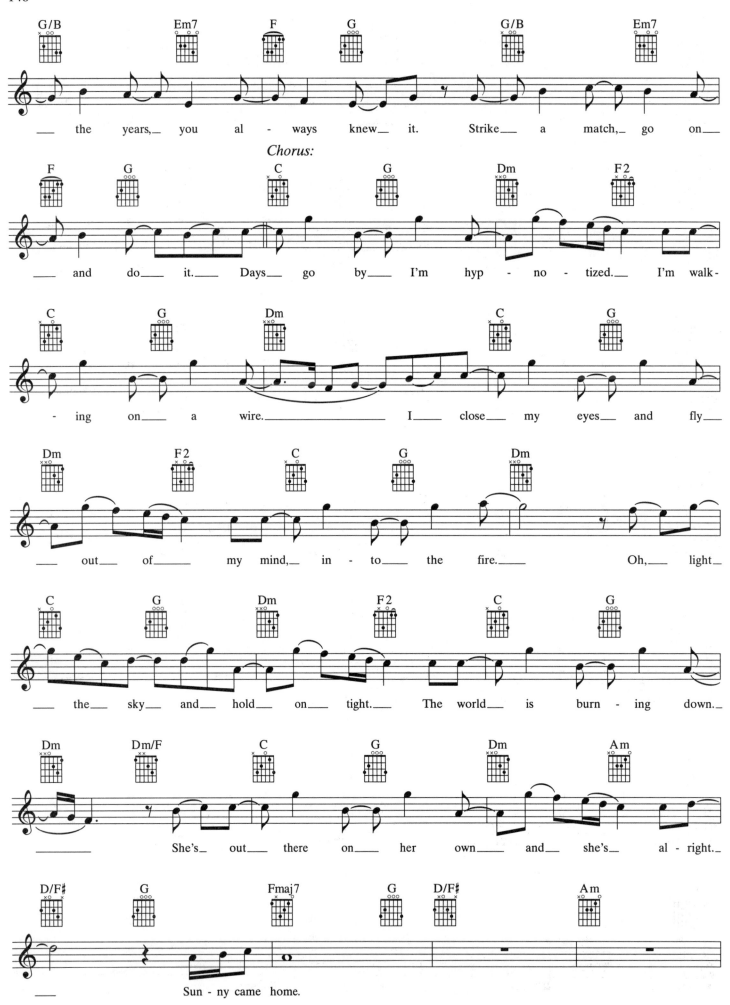

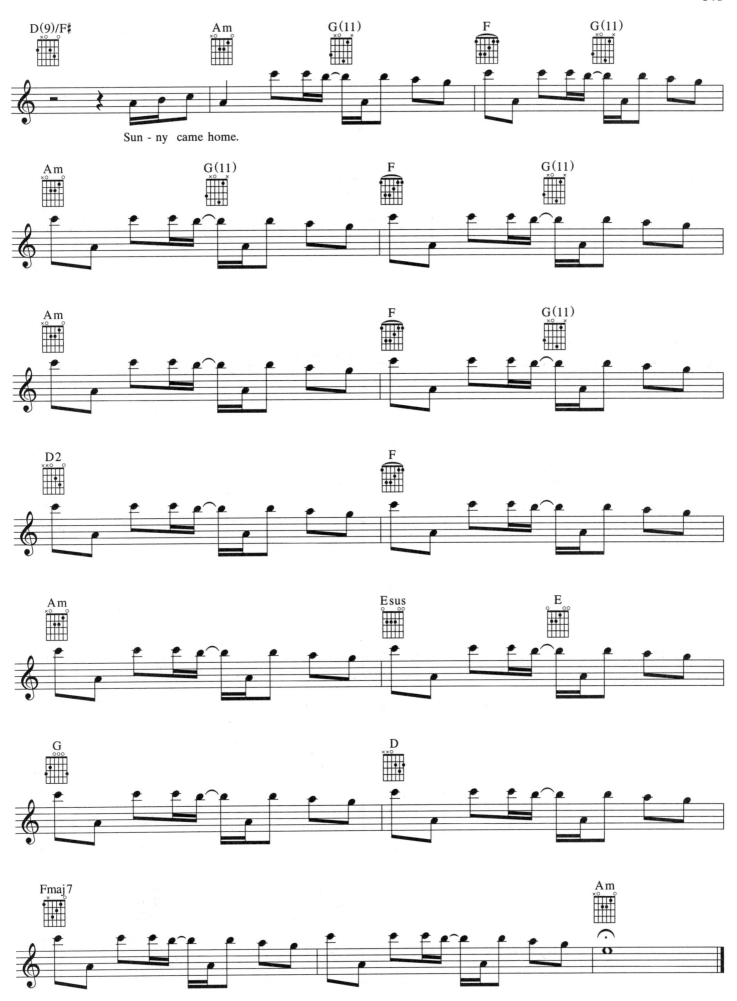

Sun - ny came home.

TEARS IN HEAVEN

Words and Music by
WILL JENNINGS and ERIC CLAPTON

Moderately slow ♩ = 80

Verses 1 & 2:

1. Would you know my name _____ if I saw you in heav-
2. Would you hold my hand _____ if I saw you in heav-

en? Would you be the same _____ if I saw you in heav-
en? Would you help me stand _____ if I saw you in heav-

en? I must be strong_ and car-ry on,___
en? I'll find my way___ through night and day,___

___ 'cause I know_ I don't be-long_____ here in heav-en.
___ 'cause I know_ I just can't stay_____ here in heav-en.

Bridge:

Time can bring you down,_ time can bend your knees._

© 1992 BLUE SKY RIDER SONGS (BMI) and DRUMLIN' LTD. (PRS)
All Rights Administered by RONDOR MUSIC (LONDON) LTD. (PRS) on behalf of BLUE SKY RIDER SONGS/
IRVING MUSIC, INC. (BMI) Administers in the U.S. and Canada
All Rights Reserved

STAY (I MISSED YOU)

Words and Music by
LISA LOEB

Folk rock ♩ = 80

Verse 1:

Guitar capo 6

You say— I on-ly hear what I want to.

And you say— I talk so all the time, so.—

And I thought what I felt was sim-ple, and I thought that I don't be-long.—

And now— that— I am— leav-ing,— now I know that I did some-thing wrong 'cause I

missed you. Yeah,_____ I missed you.

Verse 2:

And you say— I on-ly hear what I want to; I don't lis-ten hard, I don't pay at-ten-tion to the

Stay (I Missed You) - 3 - 1
GFM0001

© 1993 Songs of Universal, Inc. Furiouse Rose Music (BMI)
All Rights Administered by Songs of Universal, Inc.
All Rights Reserved

THAT DON'T IMPRESS ME MUCH

Words and Music by
SHANIA TWAIN and R.J. LANGE

© 1997 Universal - Songs Of PolyGram International, Inc., Loon Echo Inc. (BMI)
and Out Of Pocket Productions Ltd. (ASCAP)
All Rights for Out Of Pocket Productions Ltd. Controlled by Zomba Enterprises Inc. for the U.S. and Canada
All Rights for Loon Echo Inc. Controlled by Universal - Songs Of PolyGram International, Inc.
All Rights Reserved

That Don't Impress Me Much - 3 - 1
GFM0001

148

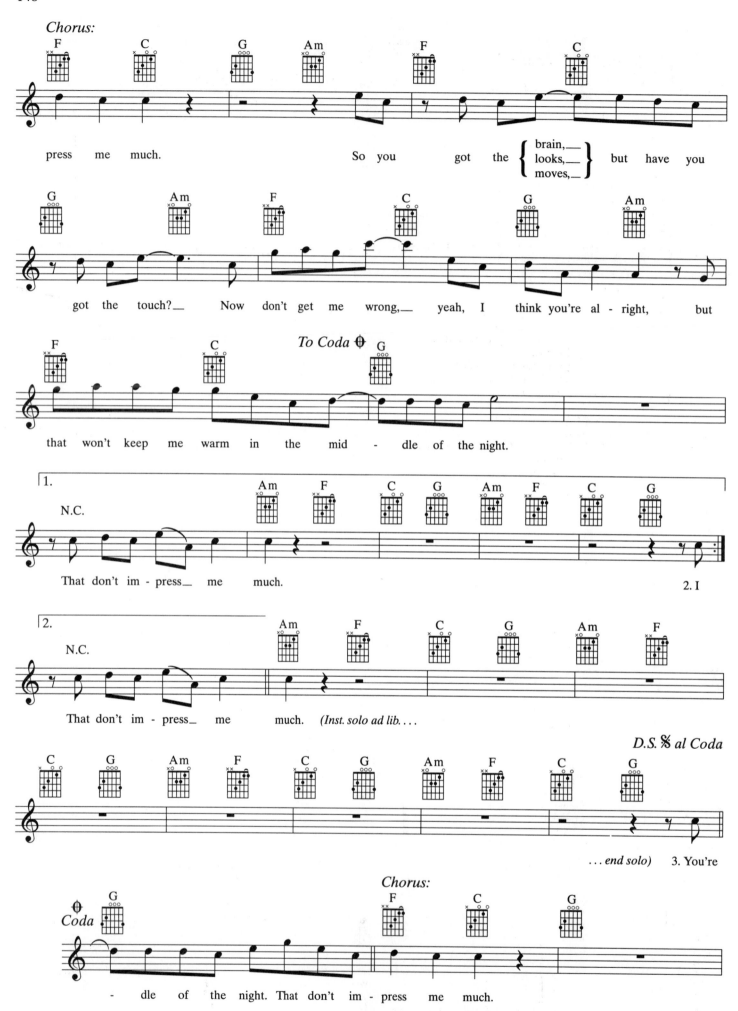

You think you're cool,__ but have you got the touch?__ Now, now don't get me wrong,__ yeah, I

think you're al - right, but that won't keep me warm on the long,_____ cold,__

lone - ly nights.__ That don't im - press__ me

much. *Instrumental solo*

(Spoken:) OK, so what do you think, you're Elvis or something? Whatever.

That don't im - press__ me.

Verse 2:
I never knew a guy who carried a mirror in his pocket
And a comb up his sleeve, just in case.
And all that extra hold gel in your hair oughta a lock it,
'Cause heaven forbid it should fall outta place.
Oh, oh, you think you're special.
Oh, oh, you think you're something else.
(Spoken:) OK, so you're Brad Pitt.
(To Chorus:)

Verse 3:
You're one of those guys who likes to shine his machine.
You make me take off my shoes before you let me get in.
I can't believe you kiss your car good-night.
Come on, baby, tell me, you must be jokin', right?
Oh, oh, you think you're something special.
Oh, oh, you think you're something else.
(Spoken:) OK, so you've got a car.
(To Chorus:)

TICK TOCK

Words and Music by
JERRY LYNN WILLIAMS, NILE RODGERS
and JIMMIE VAUGHAN

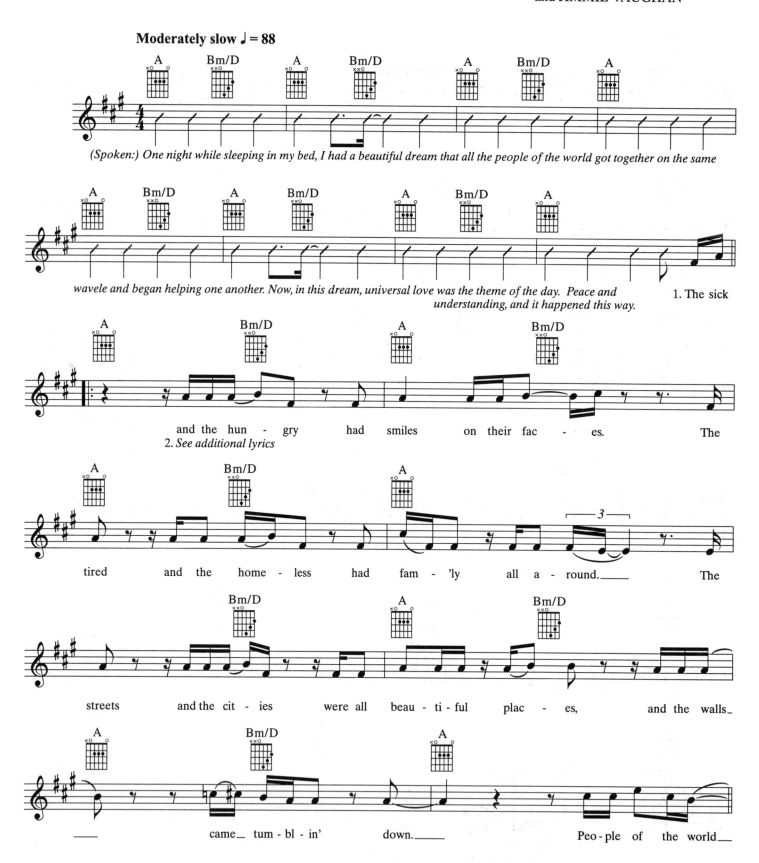

Moderately slow ♩ = 88

(Spoken:) One night while sleeping in my bed, I had a beautiful dream that all the people of the world got together on the same

wavele and began helping one another. Now, in this dream, universal love was the theme of the day. Peace and understanding, and it happened this way.

1. The sick

and the hun - gry had smiles on their fac - es. The
2. *See additional lyrics*

tired and the home - less had fam - 'ly all a - round.____ The

streets and the cit - ies were all beau - ti - ful plac - es, and the walls_

____ came_ tum - bl - in' down.____ Peo - ple of the world_

© 1990 Universal - Songs of PolyGram International, Inc., R Mode Music,
Tommy Jymi, Inc. and Red Brazos Music, Inc.
All Rights Reserved

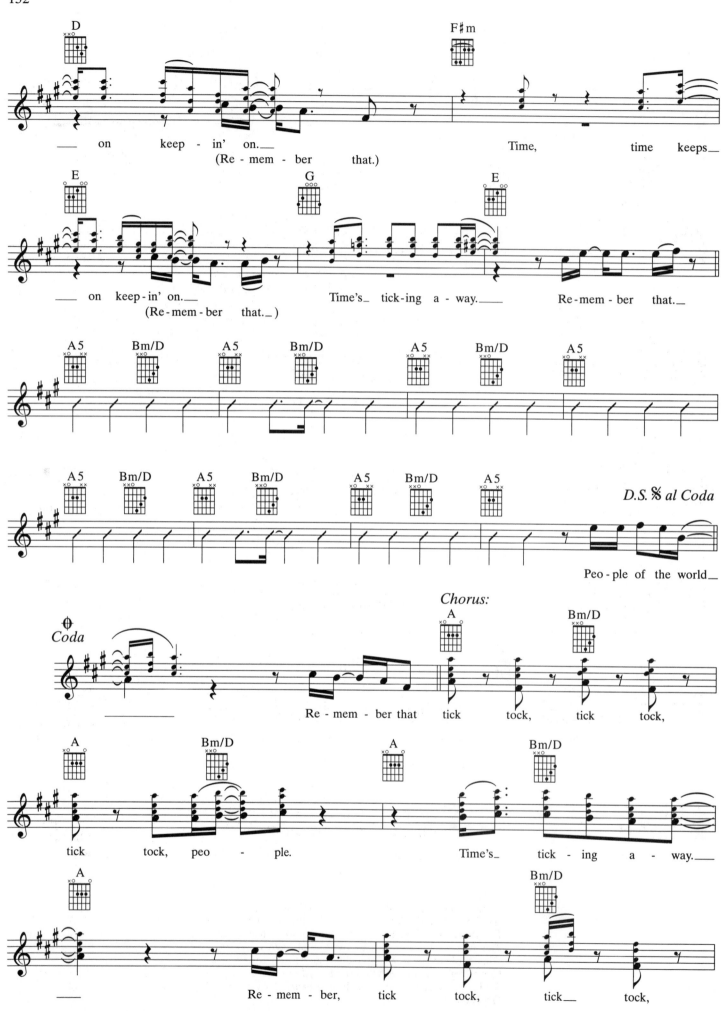

Verse 2:
I had a vision of blue skies from sea to shining sea.
All the trees in the forest stood strong and tall again.
Ev'rything was clean and pretty and safe for you and me.
The worst of enemies became the best of friends.
Oh, people of the world all had it together,
Had it together for the boys and the girls.
And the children of the world look forward to a future.
(To Chorus:)

FROM THIS MOMENT ON

Words and Music by
SHANIA TWAIN and R.J. LANGE

From This Moment On - 3 - 1
GFM0001

© 1997 Universal - Songs Of PolyGram International, Inc., Loon Echo Inc. (BMI)
and Out Of Pocket Productions Ltd. (ASCAP)
All Rights for Out Of Pocket Productions Ltd. Controlled by Zomba Enterprises Inc. (ASCAP) for the U.S. and Canada
All Rights for Loon Echo Inc. Controlled by Universal - Songs Of PolyGram International, Inc.
All Rights Reserved

TIL I HEAR IT FROM YOU

Words and Music by
JESSE VALENZUELA, ROBIN WILSON
and MARSHALL CRENSHAW

1. I did-n't ask,___ they should-n't have told___ ___ me. At first I laughed,_ but now___ it's sink-ing in___ fast,___ ___ what-ev-er they sold___ me. Well, ba - by, I don't wan-na

2. It gets___ hard,___ the mem-o-ry's fad-___ -ed. Who gets what___ they say?___ It's like - ly___ they're___ ___ just jeal-ous and jad - ed. Well, may - be I don't wan-na

Chorus:

take ad-vice___ from fools.___ I'll just fig-ure ev-'ry-thing___ is cool___

© 1995 WB MUSIC CORP., BONNEVILLE SALT FLATS MUSIC, RUTLE CORPS MUSIC,
NEW REGENCY MUSIC and AMALGAMATED CONSOLIDATED MUSIC
All Rights on behalf of BONNEVILLE SALT FLATS MUSIC and
RUTLE CORPS MUSIC Administered by WB MUSIC CORP.
All Rights Reserved

158

Til I Hear It From You - 3 - 3
GFM0001

WALKIN' ON THE SUN

Words and Music by
STEVE HARWELL, GREGORY CAMP,
PAUL DeLISLE and KEVIN COLEMAN

*Recording sounds a half-step lower than written.

© 1997 WARNER-TAMERLANE PUBLISHING CORP. and SMASH MOUTH
All Rights Reserved

Verse 2:
Twenty-five years ago they spoke out
And they broke out of recession and oppression.
And together they toked and they folked out with guitars
Around a bonfire, just singin' and clappin'; man, what the hell happened?
Yeah, some were spellbound, some were hell bound,
Some, they fell down and some got back up and fought back against the meltdown.
And their kids were hippie chicks, all hypocrites
Because their fashion is smashin' the true meaning of it.
(To Chorus:)

WHO WILL SAVE YOUR SOUL

Words and Music by
JEWEL KILCHER

Who Will Save Your Soul - 3 - 1
GFM0001

© 1996 WB MUSIC CORP. and WIGGLY TOOTH MUSIC
All Rights Administered by WB MUSIC CORP.
All Rights Reserved

164

WHAT I AM

Words and Music by
EDIE BRICKELL, KENNETH WITHROW,
JOHN HOUSER, JOHN BUSH and ALAN ALY

© 1988 Universal - Geffen Music, Edie Brickell Songs,
Withrow Publishing, Enlightened Kitty Music and Strange Mind Productions
All Rights Controlled and Administered by Universal - Geffen Music
All Rights Reserved

WHEN I COME AROUND

Words by
BILLIE JOE

Music by
BILLIE JOE,
TRÉ COOL and MIKE DIRNT

© 1994 WB MUSIC CORP. and GREEN DAZE MUSIC
All Rights Administered by WB MUSIC CORP.
All Rights Reserved

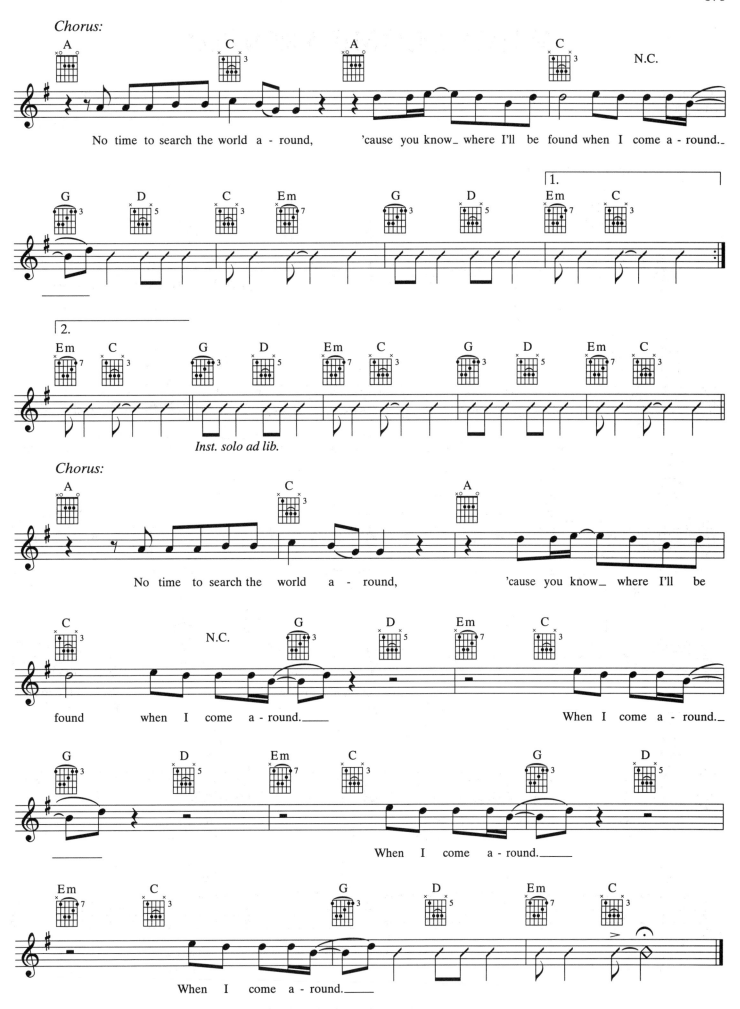

YOU LEARN

Lyrics by
ALANIS MORISSETTE

Music by
ALANIS MORISSETTE and
GLEN BALLARD

Moderately slow ♩ = 86

Guitar capo 1

mf

Oo,_____ oo,_____ ow. Oo._____

Verse:

1. I_____ rec-om-mend get-tin' your heart tram-pled on__ to
2. *See additional lyrics*

an-y-one,___ yeah,___ oh. I_____ rec-om-

mend walk-in' a-round na-ked in your liv-in' room,_____ yeah.____

Swal-low___ it down.__ (What a jag-ged lit-tle pill.___) It feels___ so good__

3. *See additional lyrics*

© 1995 Songs of Universal., Inc, Vanhurst Place, Universal - MCA Music Publishing,
A Division of Universal Studios, Inc. and Aerostation Corporation
All Rights for Vanhurst Place Controlled and Administered by Songs of Universal, Inc.
All Rights for Aerostation Corporation Controlled and Administered by
Universal - MCA Music Publishing, A Division of Universal Studios, Inc.
All Rights Reserved

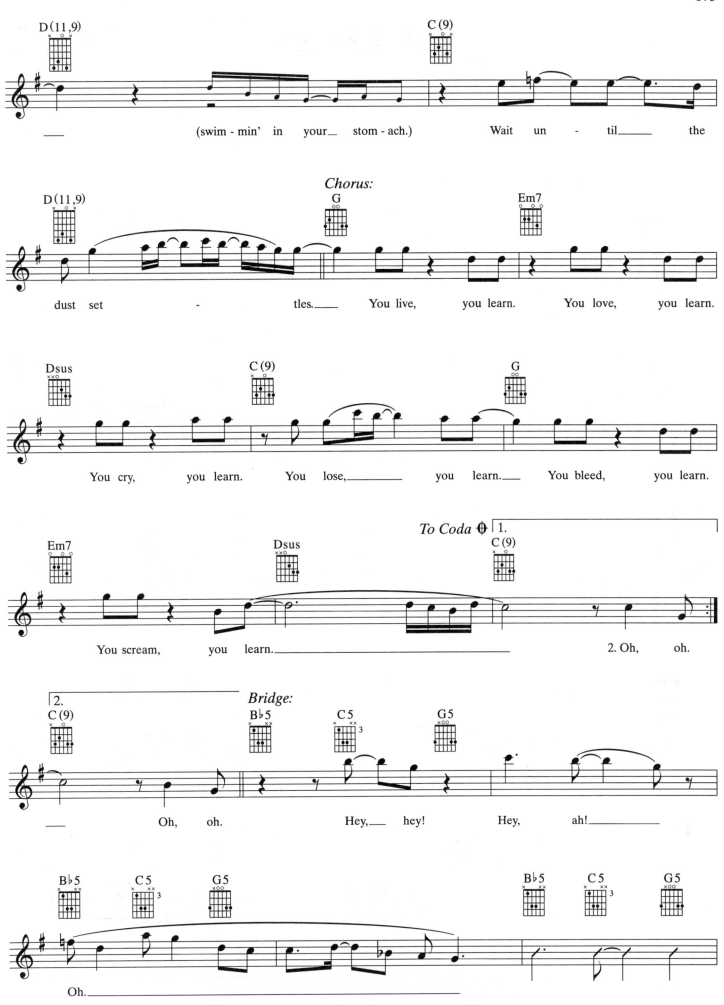

Chorus:

You grieve, you learn. You choke, you learn.

You laugh, you learn. You choose,_____ you learn.___ You pray, you learn.

You ask, you learn. You live, you learn._____

Freely

Ah.

Verse 2:
Oh, oh. I recommend biting off more than you can chew to anyone.
I certainly do, oh.
I recommend stickin' your foot in your mouth at anytime.
Feel free.
Throw it down. (The caution blocks you from the wind.)
Hold it up (to the rays).
You waited and see when the smoke clears.
(To Chorus:)

Verse 3:
Wear it out (the way a three year old would do).
Melt it down, (you're gonna have to eventually, anyway).
The fire trucks are comin' up around the bend.
(To Chorus:)

YOU OUGHTA KNOW

Lyrics by
ALANIS MORISSETTE

Music by
ALANIS MORISSETTE and GLEN BALLARD

Moderately ♩ = 104

Verse:

(N.C. 1x)

1. I want you____ to know that I'm hap-py____ for you.
2. *See additional lyrics*

I wish noth - ing but the best____ for____ you both. An old-er

(1x - tutti)

ver - sion of me, is she per - vert - ed like____ me? Would she go

down on you in____ a the-a-tre? Does she speak el - o - quent-ly, and would she

have your ba - by? I'm sure she'd make a real-ly ex - cel - lent moth-er. 1.2. 'Cause the

love that you gave, that we made was-n't a - ble to make it e-nough for you to be o -
(3.) joke that you laid in the bed, that was me, and I'm not gon-na fade as soon as you close

© 1995 Songs of Universal, Inc., Vanhurst Place, Universal - MCA Music Publishing,
A Division of Universal Studios, Inc. and Aerostation Corporation
All Rights for Vanhurst Place Controlled and Administered by Songs of Universal, Inc.
All Rights for Aerostation Corporation Controlled and Administered by
Universal - MCA Music Publishing, A Division of Universal Studios, Inc.
All Rights Reserved

You Oughta Know - 3 - 1
GFM0001

176

Ah.

Ah.

Ah.

Ah.

Ah.

Ah.

D.S. ℅ al Coda

Ah. Ah. Ah. Ah. Ah. 3. 'Cause the

Coda

ought - a know. I'm here to re - mind you of the mess

you left when you went a - way. It's not fair to de - ny me of the cross

N.C.

I bear that you gave to me. You, you, you ought - a know.

Verse 2:
You seem very well, things look peaceful.
I'm not quite as well, I thought you should know.
Did you forget about me, Mister Duplicity?
I hate to bug you in the middle of dinner.
It was a slap in the face, how quickly I was replaced
And are you thinking of me when you f∗∗∗ her?
'Cause the love you gave, that we made
Wasn't able to make it enough for you to be open wide, no.
And everytime you speak her name, does she know
How you told me you'd hold me until you died, 'til you died.
But you're still alive. And I'm here...
(To Chorus:)

You Oughta Know - 3 - 3
GFM0001

YOU WERE MEANT FOR ME

Words and Music by
JEWEL KILCHER and STEVE POLTZ

Moderate swing feel ♩ = 118

Verse:

1. I hear the clock, it's six A. M., I feel so far from
2.3. *See additional lyrics*

*Recording sounds a half-step lower than written.

where I've been. I've got my eggs and my pan-cakes, too,

I've got ma-ple syr-up, ev-'ry-thing but you. I break the yolks and make a

smil-y face, I kind of like it in my brand new place. I wipe the

spots a-bove the mirror, don't leave the keys in the door. I *nev-er put wet towels* on the

You Were Meant for Me - 3 - 1
GFM0001

© 1995 WB MUSIC CORP., WIGGLY TOOTH MUSIC and POLIO BOY
All Rights on behalf of WIGGLY TOOTH MUSIC Administered by WB MUSIC CORP.
All Rights Reserved

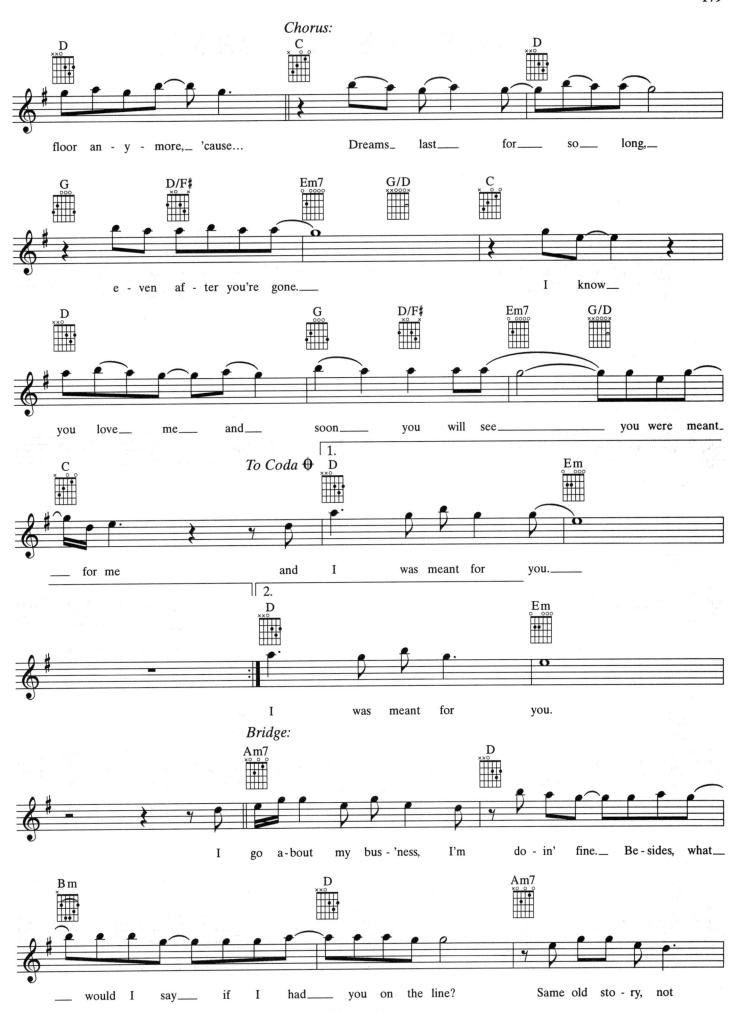

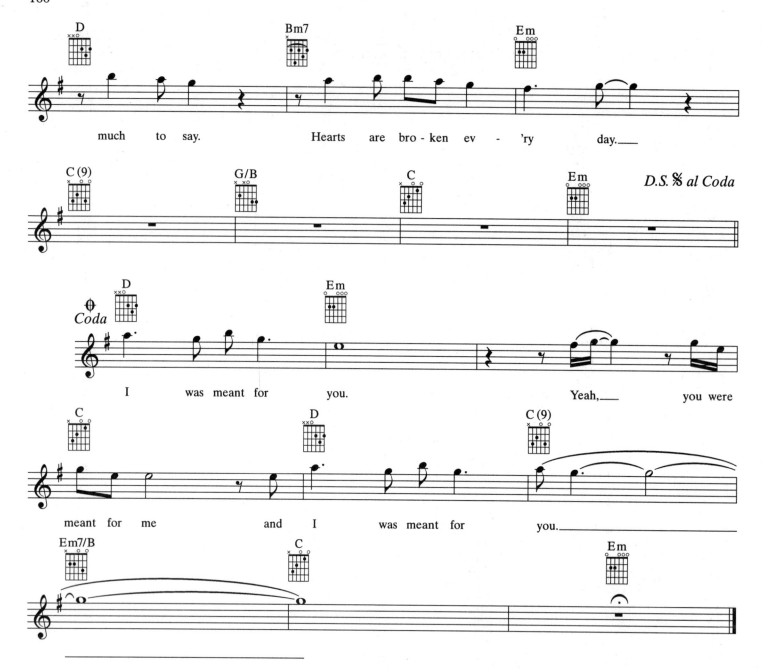

much to say. Hearts are bro - ken ev - 'ry day.___

D.S. ℅ al Coda

Coda

I was meant for you. Yeah,___ you were

meant for me and I was meant for you.___

Verse 2:
I called my mama, she was out for a walk.
Consoled a cup of coffee, but it didn't wanna talk.
So I picked up a paper, it was more bad news,
More hearts being broken or people being used.
Put on my coat in the pouring rain.
I saw a movie, it just wasn't the same,
'Cause it was happy and I was sad,
And it made me miss you, oh, so bad.
(To Chorus:)

Verse 3:
I brush my teeth and put the cap back on,
I know you hate it when I leave the light on.
I pick a book up and then I turn the sheets down,
And then I take a breath and a good look around.
Put on my pj's and hop into bed.
I'm half alive but I feel mostly dead.
I try and tell myself it'll be all right,
I just shouldn't think anymore tonight.
(To Chorus:)